# Junius Over Far

CHARLOTTE ZOLOTOW BOOK

## ALSO BY VIRGINIA HAMILTON

Zeely

The House of Dies Drear

The Time-Ago Tales of Jahdu

The Planet of Junior Brown

W.E.B. Du Bois: A Biography

Time-Ago Lost: More Tales of Jahdu

M.C. Higgins, the Great

Paul Robeson: The Life and Times of a Free Black Man

The Writings of W.E.B. Du Bois

Arilla Sun Down

Justice and Her Brothers

Dustland

The Gathering

Jahdu

Sweet Whispers, Brother Rush

The Magical Adventures of Pretty Pearl

Willie Bea and the Time the Martians Landed

A Little Love

Virginia Hamilton

Junius
Over
Far

Harper & Row, Publishers

Acknowledgement

Lyrics from "Stone Free," "The Wind Cries, Mary," "Purple Haze,"
and "Foxey Lady" by Jimi Hendrix reprinted through courtesy
of Bella Godiva Music, Inc. No other reproductions allowed
without authorization from Bella Godiva Music, Inc.

Library of Congress Cataloging in Publication Data
Hamilton, Virginia.
    Junius over far.

    "A Charlotte Zolotow book."
    Summary: After his aged and mentally deteriorating
grandfather leaves his family to return to his home
island in the Caribbean, fourteen-year-old Junius
decides to follow him and witnesses his island heritage
while rescuing his grandfather from a dangerous
situation.
    [1. Grandfathers—Fiction.    2. Caribbean Area—
Fiction]    I. Title.
PZ7.H1828Jt    1985      [Fic]        84-48344
ISBN 0-06-022194-1
ISBN 0-06-022195-X (lib. bdg.)

1 2 3 4 5 6 7 8 9 10
First Edition
First American Edition

*To The Children of the Sun*
*To Jaime and Leigh*

# Junius Over Far

# One

Junius headed directly home from school, as usual. Where was he to go, walking in this icy, late November?

"Junius. Jun-i-ahs? Wear your muffler!" his mother had called to him as he left the house this past morning.

"Muhtha, nobody wear no muffla like that here. *Please*," he had answered, naturally falling into the lilting, Caribbean accent of his grandfather, Jackabo.

"Junius! You'll catch cold."

"Please!" Junius had hollered. "Good day, Muhtha. It does not be that cold this *marnin'*." And he had leaped the steps from the front porch. He had loped to school in his long, swinging stride. His thin, scarcely muscled legs seemed to start somewhere above his hips as they pulled him smoothly along the streets.

Junius Rawlings was tall and lean, almost five feet eleven inches already. And he was not yet fifteen years old.

Now it was afternoon and after school, and he moved agilely out of the area, gliding behind the other students in a rhythm all his own. Good that there was sun shining brightly. But it was a cold sun, no warmth anywhere.

"Junie-mahn, when you goin' out for basketball?" the students often called after him in the halls. It was only in the low hallways that they seemed to notice him. "Come on, Junie-mahn, play ball and give this sorry high school a break!"

But Junius had hung his head. When the gym teacher, who was also the junior varsity basketball coach, had smiled longingly at him, Junius had turned away. How could he play sports when his grandfather was there at home, needing him, waiting for him at the end of each school day?

*Quickly, Junius son!* Junius could summon Grandfather Jackabo at any time at all. *I have one thing of great importance to show you this day.* The softly accented tones of voice: *wan theeng of gret eempor-tahnce.*

Grandfather. Wearing the muffler that now belonged to Junius. It had been one of two concessions Grandfather had made to the chill of North America.

Junius shivered as he followed on the heels of students on their way from school. Unusual that they must head right into the weather. The cold wind most often swept across the high school campus at their backs. He wished he had worn the great black muffler now. A cold, damp east wind stung his eyes and made them water. Junius was hatless and without a scarf. No gloves. Tears of cold glistened on his cheeks. His neck was freezing above his collar.

At the corner across from Bethune High School all the students crowded in bunches before going their separate ways into the west-end neighborhoods or on east. Heading into the downtown area for malts or hot chocolate at Mary and Slim's. The place was a counter-and-eight-booth luncheonette sandwiched between the drugstore and the variety store on the main street. The high school students hung out at Mary and Slim's for hours. But it had been Junius' custom to let them go on when he reached his corner, with Grandfather swaying there a half block in, freezing himself and eagerly searching for Junius.

Grandfather Jackabo! The beige, tuniclike cloak made of monk's cloth flowed around him. His black muffler was looped twice around his neck, with both ends flung over his shoulders. The lengths of wool hung down his slightly curved back nearly to his ankles like soft, ebony wings. His staff, a bamboo pole, rested against his left shoulder; and with his left hand he held on to it for support. With his free hand Grandfather Jackabo would wave Junius to him. That far away, Junius had seen Grandfather's black eyes shining at him. His bald head had a reddish-brown sheen that seemed to glow in the cold.

Oh, the sight of him, old, black son of the islands! Completely bowlegged, he wore black wool leggings he had knitted himself. So had he knitted the muffler, old island mahn. But he was gone now.

The kids would whoop loudly when they saw Grandfather Jackabo waiting. But that was all they did. Never had they been nasty to Junius concerning his grandfather.

They weren't being mean or malicious now, as the last bunch of kids paused to notice Junius. Perhaps out of boredom with one another, or the east wind, they discovered he was there.

They had just reached Junius' corner and peered down the block, noting that Grandfather was nowhere to be seen. They had not quite gotten used to the fact that he was not there. But old Jackabo's absence now reminded them that Junius was among them.

"Hey-mahn is here! Junie-mahn! Come here, Hey-mahn!" someone cried out, using his two nicknames in a high, sweet voice. A beautiful young woman detached herself from the group at Junius' corner. She was Sarrietta Dobbs. She flung herself playfully at Junius after setting her books on the sidewalk. "Oh, Hey-mahn, you coming with us?" "Hey-mahn" was her own personal nickname for him, which other girls had taken up. It came from the fact that he would greet other guys with "Hey, mahn!" to say good morning. Guys always called him Junie-mahn.

Sarrietta hugged him around his middle. He stood, paralyzed, holding his books high above her head. He was stunned that she had thrown herself at him in such a way.

Truly, she does love me, Junius thought. I wonder if I should write Grandfahtha, tell him I have a love.

Kids were laughing, watching from the corner. Junius supposed they were laughing at his happiness, his adoration for beautiful Sarrietta.

"Hey, Junie-mahn, I wish she'd throw her arms around me like that," Henry Smith said. "I'd sure know what to do about it, too."

"Shut up, Plas, you're not sweet like Hey-mahn is," Sarrietta said.

Plas, for Plastic Wrap, was Henry's nickname. Henry was so light complexioned, Junius sometimes imagined, as did the others, that he could see right through him. They all had nicknames. Sarrietta was sometimes Sugar Dobbs, or "Shoog," but not to Junius. "Come on, go with us, Hey-mahn," Sarrietta urged. "Now your grandfather's gone back to the islands, you got nothing to do half the time, you know you don't." Teasing him. She swayed him from side to side.

Every school day Junius fell in love with Sarrietta Dobbs all over again. Her smoky brown eyes. Her perfect, burnt-chocolate coloring, much like Grandfather's and his own coloring, but richer somehow. She sang in the choir at his church. He would forget her in the busy time when he studied his books, played the music of the islands that Grandfather had taught him, and also what he called the "warrior music" he tried playing on his guitar. She was an *older* girl, was the way Junius thought of Sarrietta. They had some classes together.

I do not feel much like I belong, was a thought often in Junius' mind, as it was now.

He felt so much younger. There was more to this feeling, of course. And every time Sarrietta paid attention to him, as she did now, he grew tongue-tied.

"Come on, Hey-mahn!" Sarrietta said, whispering up at him. She released him to retrieve her books. Then she grabbed his hand again, pulling him along.

Bette Ann Bell detached herself from the group and came running over. She clutched Junius' arm full of books.

"Come on, Hey-mahn, buy me a Coke!" she said.

"No, ma'am," Sarrietta said. "He's coming with me, Duncey—I invited him."

"He's comin' with me, too," Bette Ann "Duncey" Bell said. "I invite him too."

They pulled him along, back to the group. Junius felt only the touch of Sarrietta, her hand holding his hand.

And then, as quickly as things had been good for Junius, they turned not so good. Plas took Sarrietta's hand away from Junius. He grabbed her and held her tightly to his chest, books and all. He whispered in her ear. She giggled against him. She seemed not to be trying to get loose from him.

[6]

How good-looking Plas was! Junius thought. I could not do somethin' like that, ever. Making myself to touch and to hold Sarrietta!

His difference from the other older guys struck him hard then.

"What he saying to Sarrietta? What he saying to her!" Terry "Slam" Edwards said about Plas' whisperings.

"I'm tellin' her," Plas said, "Sugar Dobbs got a date with me after the game Friday night. I'm tellin' her, Sugar Dobbs goin' to the dance with me after that."

"No, I didn't say I would!" Sarrietta said, struggling to break free, but not hard enough, it seemed to Junius.

"I'm not gonna let you loose until you say you goin' to the dance with me," Plas said.

If I could ask her to the dahnce, Junius thought, maybe she would go with me.

Duncey Bell let Junius loose. That made him feel awful. Since Sarrietta didn't want him, he supposed Duncey would say, then she didn't want him either.

Why was it girls were so unkind toward him, he wondered. Did they believe he had no feelings? He hung his head.

As quickly as he had been the center of attention, Junius was now out in the wind alone. Walking on the outside of the group all by himself. Plas held Sarrietta to him. They had long passed Junius' corner. Now he would have to continue on downtown, even though his face was numb, his neck like a bar of ice.

Well, I will do it, he thought, shrugging his shoulders. I will sit there with them. What else is there for me to do, with Grandfahtha Jackabo gone such a distance away?

Grandfahtha! Why did you not take me with you? Why did you have to go all at once, when before you did not have to go? When there was no thinking of going, not once.

Junius felt the pain of loss inside.

All the time you telling me tales, he thought. Showing me about the lost continent—Antilles, you called it—you were longing for the islands, yes?

Junius shifted his books; his chin was deep in his overcoat for warmth.

Wastin' away from homesickness. Yes, you were, Grandfahtha. I see that now. But you should have waited. Grandfahtha, I would go with you. I would take care of you, old mahn of the islands. Gettin' decrepit, you should not be wanderin' about by yourself.

Junius smiled wanly to himself. But . . . you left me here. Sadly, he shook his head. And shifting his books, he put one hand in his coat pocket to warm it, then the other. The voices of the students noisily hurrying through the cold streets grew distant.

Junius was remembering. Grandfather, studying the great round globe on its stand that he plugged in each day. It would glow with light, spotlighting Grandfather's dark face, bathing it red. Then Grandfather would study the little dots of the Caribbean. They were the island countries, one in particular that he loved.

"Greater Antilles," Grandfather called the islands. And "Lesser Antilles, the Leewards, the Windwards. Here is my island," he would say. "The land of the snake." Grandfather pronounced snake as *sneck*. "Snake Island," he said, pronouncing it *Sneck Eye-lahn*. "Hee, hee," Grandfather laughed. "Tis a joke, Junius, dontcha know. Snake Island has no snakes! But it tis shaped like a snake. Ha, ha!

"Junius son," Grandfather saying, tapping one tiny, almost invisible dot in particular upon the glowing globe. "You go there, never think the manchineel is some apple tree. My Gawd, no! The Spanish live there, they say *manzanillo*. The French live there, they say *mancenille*. Any way you say it, that tree poison you, Junius son. The little yellow-green fruit no apples. Milky juice, no apple juice. Long ago, the Carib native peoples fought they enemy by using arrows dipped in deadly manchineel sap, dontcha know, son.

"No, Junius son," Grandfather saying on, "you go to that beach. Mahn, lie down under the old manchineel. Hang the towel there on he low, twisted branch. But never you eat of the old manchineel, touch of him. Never ever you do that, Junius son."

Junius sighed. Walking, striding, he felt little cold now. There was worse hurting than cold, late November wind.

The globe of the world no longer glowed with light

[9]

in Grandfather's room. No longer did pirates come alive on its surface, as over the years the island dots had grown large in Junius' mind as he grew up.

"There were slaves, planters, and privateers," Grandfather had explained. He knew the islands, he said; although it seemed to Junius, as he grew older, that Grandfather confused their history. For Grandfather Jackabo, that history had become one continuous stream flowing without beginning or end.

The globe of the world was a gray, shadowy ball unlit in a silent room now. In Grandfather Jackabo's empty room.

I am one sad grandson of the island mahn this day, Junius thought. He grinned suddenly. They were on the main street already. Junius by himself, the group walking in front of him. He was close enough to hear them tease and laugh.

In the restaurant packs of students took over, as they did each day. By the time Junius paused to figure out where to sit, the booths were full. He went to the counter and sat on a stool, right after which the counter area filled with students. It was an end stool Junius had; he could turn sideways and be near the booth where Sarrietta and her friends sat. Junius watched them for a while. Studied Sarrietta's profile. Those in the booth were busy with talk, giggling laughter, ordering malts. The chatter in the small restaurant rose to a raucous pitch.

The counterwoman, Mrs. Teally, slapped a glass of

water before Junius. Hard of hearing, she turned her hearing aid down even further against the din. She went down the line of the counter, pad in hand, taking orders by reading lips. Junius said nothing. Mrs. Teally didn't seem to notice. He drank the water down. Then he got up easily, pretending he was in a hurry. He hoped perhaps the others would see him leave and call him back. But he was at the door. He paused to let them call his name—*Hey-mahn, where you goin' wit' your bad self, chal? Stay awhile, Junie-mahn.* The noise was loud.

Tinkling bells showered him as he held the door open. The sound reminded him of Christmas. A swift vision of Grandfather making island "okra fungi," the delicious ball-shaped cornmeal pudding served with boiled fish and onion sauce.

And feeding it to Junius, a small boy then. Grandfather's arm around him, whispering secrets to him. No more.

Junius left.

# Two

Old Jackabo dreamed he rode a leatherback sea turtle weighing a thousand pounds. How it made him laugh! Ahhh! Hee-hee! He could feel the massive reptile sway its half ton beneath him as it cruised just under the water's surface. He dreamed he sat in a saddle on the turtle's spotted yellow shell in a sea up to his waist. Jackabo's protruding belly, shining like a cooking pot, was in the lead through the turquoise ocean. It hurt!

"Slow down, mahn, Nulio," Jackabo called to the turtle. Nulio was its name. "You go make me two Jackabos in no time, son."

"Got to be goin', Grandfahtha," said the leatherback. "It time for school, dontcha see?"

"School? Where school, turtle-mahn?" asked Jackabo.

"School which goin' down," Nulio answered.

"Where be school which goin' down, son?" asked

Jackabo. He spoke in rhythm with the leatherback's swaying through the sea swells.

"Be home." Nulio turned to look at Jackabo. Then he dived, dived into the wavering, soft light of the silent ocean deep, carrying old Jackabo with him.

I will drown, was Grandfather Jackabo's last thought. In the dream he could not swim. The salt sea stung his open, staring eyes. It pressed hard against his eardrums. He held tightly to the lanyard made of strong cord that was hooked inside the turtle's beak. He couldn't let go. He breathed deeply his last of waters he called the Caribbee Sea.

Grandfather Jackabo awoke with a violent start. There was a gentle swaying under him, and a queasy feeling in the empty pit of his stomach. There was rain in his face. He had been sleeping with his mouth open, and rainwater filled it. Gasping, he managed to swallow the water. His throat felt parched and the water was refreshing. Grandfather sat up, his heart pounding.

Dreamin' hard like that, no good for an old mahn, he thought.

He was in a flat-bottomed wooden fishing dory. It was the kind of no-nonsense sea-sound boat that old-timers of the island kept in good shape forever. A fishing pole and a bucket were at his side. At the bottom of the bucket was a carefully wrapped half cup of squid for bait.

A warm rain swept over the dory, soaking Grandfather. He wore the monk's-cloth cloak with three-quarter-length sleeves and scooped neck. His legs were bare. Faded green hiking shorts peeked from beneath the cloak. He had an old but razor-sharp rigging knife with a leather sheath, held to the belt loop with cord. He had leather boating sandals on his feet. He was soaked through his clothes. The rain kept coming, shrouding the space around him in mist. He picked at the wet on his skinny arms, where the skin hung like cloth and the veins beneath were pale-green ropes. That skin was burned reddish dark. It had peeled more than once since he had been on the island.

The swaying motion of the boat made him ill, suddenly. He leaned over the side of the dory and retched stomach bile into the water. His mouth filled with saliva, which he managed to swallow. Jackabo stuck his head between his knees until the nausea passed.

Sea legs taking the long time comin' back, he thought. How many times I been in this old boat now? Lots of times now, and it still make me sick, sometimes. But it tire me to make that motor go. Save the strength each day for goin' on this boat all by myself. Build them muscles, sure.

"Where am I?" he said. Turning, he saw rain march across a wide body of gray water, over him and on behind him to shadowy, moderate cliffs. There was no hard breeze, no lightning. Just the swift, clean rain of the tropics that always came before the wind with the sound of an army running in jackboots. It lasted only a few minutes. It left with a dry rustling of high breezes that were pungently scented with wet grasses. Clouds fell away and blue sky filled with sunlight peeked through. The sea changed to a smoky blue, then to a glossy, swelling turquoise.

"Where am I? Who is this, me?" Jackabo squeezed his eyes shut and shook the rain out of his ears. He rubbed his head, squeezed out his clothes. He looked all around him but he couldn't tell where he was.

Know who I am now, he thought. Does be somebody's fool, out here alone, any old fool, who there is no one like. That made him smile, grimly.

He moaned, leaned back down on the seat. Best to lie still, not sit up or have any movin' around. Never try to think it through. Let that cotton darkness in my head turn the corner, oh, yea, he thought. Be a beacon light there beyond the corner. I be able to see myself then. He waited for the darkness to march around. Thinking thoughts in order helped it along.

Goin' out in this boat over and over, he thought. I do remember that.

But the cotton black took its time.

"I'm an old citizen, what can be expected of me?" he said to the sky.

The day lightened around him. As it did, the mist of the rain lifted. At that moment a veil of forgetfulness moved off. Jackabo remembered something.

"Yea! Ha!" he crowed. He maneuvered to the prow of the dory, guarding the strength restored by sleep. He was careful not to rock the boat more than necessary. There were two small doors that opened under the prow.

"Food. I knew it. Leftover, better second time. I remember!" Dark cotton fell away somewhat. The corner was nearly reached and soon would come the light.

"Don't push, old fool," he told himself, reaching for a small, black pot. "It will be back." His mind. "It always will."

In the pot was okra fungi. Jackabo had made it himself a night ago to serve the old white fool, Burten Rawlings. Burtie and Jackabo were distant relatives of sorts since the time a permanent settlement of slaves was established on the island. Grandfather Jackabo's black connection to Burten Rawlings' white planter family made Grandfather laugh. It made Burtie Rawlings furious enough to cry. And some nights, in a drunken rage, old Burtie would cry enormous, salty tears. On those occasions he would rail at Jackabo, whom he called Stinking Black Jack.

They hated one another. Burtie cooked for the two of them because he couldn't stomach, he said, the mess Jackabo would throw together, and in exchange for even his hateful company. The okra fungi was the only dish that Jackabo could halfway cook, according to Burtie. Burtie did his share of the chores. And Jackabo paid good Social Security, American cash he had saved, for room and board, such as it was.

"Nothing like second-day okra fungi," Jackabo murmured. He dug in the pot with a wooden spoon. The pot was still warm, from the heat inside the prow. The fungi was made sweet with fish—snapper, parrot— and an onion sauce with okra.

He pulled out a canteen of the juice old Burtie called the Planter's Punch. Jackabo wasn't sure what it was made of.

"One of sour, two of sweet, three of strong, four of weak" was all that old Burtie would say about it. But Jackabo could guess, when he could remember; the sour was the lime juice. The sweet was sugar. Strong had to be rum, and the weak was water, and ice, when they had it.

The first time he had some of the brew Burtie made himself was the day after he had arrived back on the island. He and old Burtie had toasted each other's health, which had been the last decent gesture between them in days. Jackabo had drunk almost a quart of the Planter's Punch with his supper, the heat of the day on the hillside had been so fierce.

The Punch knocked him flat on his back for the better part of two days. Jackabo didn't know what was happening. He could not get up once he had fallen down. The whole room spun around him. He broke out in a cold sweat, and his dinner did not stay down. He could not get up that night to clean himself and change his clothing. From that moment on, Burtie called him Stinking Black Jack instead of his usual old Black Jack.

"You did that to me on purpose, you most yellow

heathen!" Jackabo accused Burtie. "That be the worst experience of my entire life," he cried. Old, mean Burtie had only laughed and slammed out of Jackabo's room.

Now Jackabo knew better than to have the Planter's Punch in large quantities. He had learned to sip it over the period of half a day. Even longer. And in addition to the one, two, three, four ingredients, there were bitter herbs and roots mixed in. He was certain he could taste the bitters on the back of his tongue.

He took a gentle sip from the canteen. He ate the fungi slowly but steadily until it was all gone.

"Ah, so good!" he said, rubbing his stomach. He leaned back, sighing. "Good to be home, oh yea." He looked all around. This was his island, it had to be. But on some days Jackabo wasn't sure. Sometimes, in the middle of the afternoon, like now, he had to wait a long time by himself to know he was in the right place.

I fly in the gret jet-propelled airplane, he mused. It look like a cathedral inside, with the hostesses to help you pray. I need no help. Sitting still all the way and cannot tell that plane be moving, except for the sound of them many engines. I pray, let this gret jet stay up on the thin air a little longer.

He in heaven surely answer me, Jackabo continued in his thoughts. The plane land on the big island. I see dark mountains far to our right out my window. Up close, I see the palm trees swayin' such grace.

Wonderful coconut palms! They comin' fast by as the gret plane landing.

And it pourin' rain! But the rain stop time we get inside. Just a rain of the tropics, I was reminded. Be forgettin' how sweet, how quickly, the rains. I forgot how warm and wet the air of the Caribbee. Feel the Caribbee on my skin, make that wrinkle-up skin almost young again.

After that I travel to the boat docks. Take the public small bus. He say—where you go, the driver say. And I say—I need the boat to Snake Island. Don't give me no more gret jet planes. Driver laugh. I give you *la lancha*—he say, and he do, too. I understand every word he say, although he not be speakin' like me. They come back to you, the tongues of Caribbee.

Take me over an hour to get there to another side of the big island. And there I ride the ferryboat to here. *La lancha*, the launch, the ferryboat, taken me two hours. My first taste of the sea salt in many years. Ho! I get so excited, I stand an hour by the rail. No matter to me I get soaken from the waves sprayin' all over the launch. The Caribbee is always warm so. We pass little *cayos*, little coral reefs, nobody live on. But they so pretty to look at. The white surf, licking at the hot, yellow sand soaked in the sunlight, oh yea. They, the cays, looking like some giant statues, shapes resting, cooling in the swells of Caribbee.

But supposin' the ferryboat does not be stoppin' at my island first? I feared. Then my island, it rise out of the sea. It but some dark hump at first, far away. It rises, sharpens into focus. It a shape curved on itself, dontcha see. I remember that shape in my dreams. And then it rise, a cone, a serpent head lookin' over the water. I think I do recognize it, with two smaller reef islands in its chain. We pass by the smaller islands; they are Rock Cay and Black Cay, someone down the line, leaning on the rail, says, explaining to somebody else new. Why it is Black Cay? Because of black rocks and sands, because of volcanic activity long ago, so they say. Nobody want to live there. I get on off first anyway. Supposin' this I see not my island, but somebody else's island?

But Burtie Rawlings, he right here. I write I am comin'. To Burtie Rawlings, Rawlings Estate, Snake Island. Do I remember Burtie? They so many old white souls like him, scattered everywhere, dontcha know. Like so many wet, white pots dryin' out on the way-back burners.

Nobody else know me no more here, I been gone so long. Island people move about, looking so for work. Whole islands, sometimes, leave and go again. This my last goin' somewhere, I think. Don't tell the boy, Junius son. Oh, Grandson! What old mahn want to be a burden?

But this has to be my island. I am too tired, too old to go one step farther. I mean to spend my dyin' time day and night right here.

No mahn, but some might remember me if I speak

to them who I am. Old Jackabo Rawlings be my name. They might laugh behind they hands, thinkin' of white Burtie Rawlings.

Say that to the *senora*, does be the postal clerk at the post office. Little pink-painted building, not two stories high, with the flag laying limp on its pole in front. Say it to the David Barnstable owns the one grocery. He is a black mahn of prominence. Three groceries now, scattered about the town. I never knew no groceries when I was a boy. You go to somebody's house who have flour and they sell you flour. You go to somebody's small plot of land they grow sugarcane and you trade a turn hoeing, perhaps, for the cane or the sugar. Just whatever you need, maybe you barter it. But no grocer. Someday maybe be supermarket or *supermercado*, a *super marché* here on this place, my island. Wouldn't that be somethin' now!

Thinking that, it came to Jackabo who he was and he knew it for certain, and where he had been and to what place he had come.

I am. But it frightened him that he could lose his senses so often, so easily.

Be old Jackabo, here. Be Grandfather gone over far. It was a comfort to remind himself of that. But maybe that's the trouble. Have to be too many old mahns for everybody. How is the boy doin'? Better write him one day. It tis the time to give Junius son report on me.

He chuckled. The boat trembled, as though laughing with him. He prepared to lift anchor. Jackabo had taken the boat out a ways from shore on the side of the deep harbor. The mangroves of a tiny island called Pirates' Cay were perhaps three quarters of a mile away from him, situated in the bay. The Pirates' Cay looked misty, mysterious. There were one or two sailboats deep within its thick growth of mangroves. Fishing, probably.

He had anchored the Rawlings dory to the left of the small Pelican Cove off the deep bay. He now lived on the old Rawlings estate on a steep hillside above Pelican Cove. From his vantage now, as the boat slowly swung on its anchor, he could see across the bay to the bare poles of the sloops and gaff-rigged cutters hidden in the foliage of Pirates' Cay. It took a practiced eye to separate the ships' masts from mesquite and mangrove wood through the misty light. There were no unsightly motor yachts on the deep bay this day, there being no holidays for a few weeks yet. Not many visitors to his backwater island. But the big yachts pulled in at Christmastime and New Year's time. All holidays were so gay and plentiful in the lands of the Caribbee.

Jackabo squinted around the bay, at the rim road that traversed the whole coast of the island. Nothing moved. It was afternoon, hot as Hades. Maybe he had died and had gone not to Heaven but the other route, he thought. The heat sorely tested his senses.

"Better get out of this now," he murmured. Better

not let that sun take what strength I have left, he thought. Get this dory back to Pelican Cove. Home. He sighed, hating to exchange the cooling bay for the heat of the hillside.

In a few minutes Jackabo began pulling up the anchor down in the silt and mud at the bottom. It took him time. He kept the motor shaft up out of the water to be sure not to catch his line on the propeller at the shaft's end. His muscles were pretty good now, and with effort he pulled the anchor in. Once that was taken care of, he adjusted the motor shaft and propeller to their proper position in the water. He made certain the motor was in neutral when he started it. It *putt-putt*ed a moment before it turned over and came on strong. It felt as if the boat had come to life. Pelicans, startled by the noise, lifted out of their nests along the cove, their wings flapping like the sound of leather mitts clapping.

Jackabo laughed, feeling ageless. He was certain he had become, at most, fifty years old again and in his prime in the searing sunlight. He sat down and headed the boat in. His motor was a twenty-five-horsepower Evinrude. It took him only a few minutes to get to the shore and the boat dock. Kicking up a breeze and warm spray, soaking him to his knees in salty sea.

# Three

The sorriest thing in my life does be coming on home to no*body*.

Junius, thinking to himself.

This ol' gray house, making me so sick!

A gray house, to Junius, was a house interior with no one in it. His home was actually a two-story white frame structure trimmed in red with a nice front porch. It had a red porch swing that was now raised up to the slatted ceiling on shortened chains for the winter. His mother, Jaylene, worked part-time as a school counselor every morning and in the afternoon as a volunteer in the day-care center. She was home when Junius entered; Junius needn't have been so melodramatic. She was straightening up the house, as she did after work, there being no one else to do it and no time in the morning.

"I need some day *care*, me," Junius at once complained. His mother was folding newspapers strewn about in the living room from the night before.

"I need me a volunteer, dontcha know, take care of *me*." He sounded cross even to himself. Speaking as closely as he could to Grandfather's lilting voice, although Grandfather Jackabo would never have sounded so peevish.

"Junius, son," his mother said, in greeting. Smiling at him. He got out of his overcoat, left it in a pile on the floor by the front door. He went to his mother.

"Jaylene!" he said, softly, putting his arms around her. He had to scrunch down to place his head on her shoulder.

"You brought the cold in all over me!" she said. He could feel the November outdoors envelop her, fight her warmth. Cold would lose, had to.

His mother laughed and patted his arm. She gave him a kiss on his icy cheek.

"You're grown up now!" she told him, swaying with him, reaching for his shoulders. She was only five feet two inches. Junius folded himself even more in to rest more comfortably. "You don't need me every minute," she said. "Let the little children have my company for a while."

"They little children taking his muhtha, Jaylene, from Junius son!"

"Still missing Grandfather so much?" she said, patting him. He let himself be cuddled a moment longer.

"Gone a month tomorrow. I worry about him, though," she said.

[ 25 ]

Junius straightened up. "You worry about him, but nobody do nothing about him." He let go of the sweet safety of his mother and slumped in a chair. She tidied up around him.

They had had the same discussion over and over. Truly, Junius thought, I should have this argument with Fahtha. He responsible for letting Grandfahtha go.

"Letting an old mahn like that go off thousands a miles to who knows by himself, alone," Junius fussed. "Why'd he have to go all of a sudden like that!"

"Your grandfather's not a child, Junius," she said. "And it wasn't all of a sudden. He never really liked the weather here. He thought about going many times." She sat down on the couch, holding a stack of papers in her lap.

"Muhtha, he's seventy-six years old. He got no business off by himself."

"Seventy-six isn't old, goodness, not these days," she said. "Grandfather is in good health. A little arthritis, but you know what he says about that."

Junius knew. Grandfather saying, *Oh, Gawd! Don't lettin' me sit still too long. You know the o-rahnge spiders. They gret big, big as o-rahnge fists. They comin' at night sharin' with you and growin' they webs. Sittin' too long, this old mahn look down. So suddenly—poof—he see them silver spinnin' threads. Be down he ears around the neck. He all tied up 'til he die that way. Oh, no, Gawd, no. Never stayin' in no one place too long. Arthritis! Spiders!*

"A little forgetful, maybe, at times," his mother continued, after a pause in which they remembered Grandfather. "So he's a bit eccentric—I mean, yesterdays have a way of becoming today and tomorrow for him. But that's not wrong." She thought a moment. "The arthritis was something he learned to live with. I hope he wasn't imagining he would become a burden to us. . . ."

"Eighty-year-old mahn afred of *orange* spiders—I never seen no big orange spiders," Junius went on. "Grandfahtha got no business off on his own, dontcha see?" he pleaded. "Somethin' happen there, he fall down, he not get up, who knows? Somethin' happen, the distance too great to do something for him."

"He's not alone and he's seventy-six, not eighty," his mother said. "There's a village on the island. There are people and he's not unknown there. Junius." His mother smoothed her hands on the crumpled newsprint. "Don't start me worrying, too. No, your grandfather can still take care of himself. And there's the other elderly gentleman on that old estate. They'll look after one another."

"But you don't know if all that tis true!" Junius said. "You don't know if Grandfahtha be rememberin' at all straight. Our old mahn and another old n..hn make two same, worrisome old mahns. An old white owner of a dead plantation!"

"Junius." His mother's face seemed to close over the same argument. "Our old man, as you call him, is still

[27]

a free man," she said. She looked very self-assured now. "Just because he's old, we should tell him what to do, tell him where he can and can't go? No, we have more respect for him than that. He wanted to go to his home, Junius. Remember, he lived there with his mother until he moved away with his wife. As I remember, they lived on other of the islands before they came to the States. I'm sure he is where he wants to be at this period of his life. He's doing all right."

"But when will he come back?" Junius wanted to know. He felt something close to desperation. "When will he give this up and come on back here where he belong?"

His mother gave no answer to that. She had the papers in her arms now, ready to take them away. "I think you need to dwell on other things," she said firmly. She smiled.

"I got no other 'things' to dwell on," he muttered.

"Saw you with the other students. Did you go to Mary and Slim's with them?"

Junius nodded. Her son looked troubled. Jaylene did not like that look. She had seen him on the main street as she came home from work. Yes, all by himself on the outside, left out, as usual. It hurt her. There had been a time when she thought his grandfather's influence was all to the good. But now she didn't know. Now she wondered if their affection hadn't somehow kept Junius' father from sharing in it. Junius not only talked just like the old man, but seemed to think differently from both his father and the young people around him.

She had left Junius with Jackabo all day when he was small. Left him every day because she and his father had to work. She wondered why they hadn't put him in nursery school. But then, she knew. Their thinking was that the boy and the grandfather would be good company for one another. And they were right. Junius had loved being with Jackabo; the two had adored one another. But now Junius was so old, himself, sometimes. The boy and the man grown old together. And who would have guessed that his separation from his grandfather would have affected Junius so? But she was relieved, she couldn't help it. Relieved to have Grandfather Jackabo away for a while. Now maybe Junius would make more of an effort to relate to young people his own age. And to his father, Damius, too.

"Was there mail today, Muhtha?" Junius asked suddenly.

"What? Oh, no. No, there wasn't any," she said.

"Maybe tomorrow, then," he said. "'Tis time a letter come from Grandfahtha."

"Yes, it is time," his mother said.

Grandfather had written once every week or ten days since he'd left. Long, rambling letters that somehow brought the blistering sun of the tropics into the cold north, into their house, to live in Junius' thoughts.

"Don't take everything to heart, Junius," his mother said, getting up from the couch with her pile of papers. "I know you miss Grandfather, but try to be happy for him, that he's able to do what he wants to do at his age. And I'm sure he'd want you to have a good time with your friends. Will you try?"

He got up, sighing. He nodded. "I will try, Muhtha," he said. He went over, picked up his coat that he'd left in a pile on the floor. He hung it in the closet. Then, taking up his schoolbooks, he went to his room, passing the closed door to Grandfather's room.

I will not look in, I will not see that . . . He did not finish the thought. Impulsively, Junius went inside Grandfather's room. The room was much cooler than the rest of the house, closed off by itself. Quickly, he went over to the huge globe on its stand. The stand had ball wheels. He could push the whole apparatus and it would roll.

Why did I not think of this before? Because it was so much a part of Grandfahtha. Maybe I could not separate it from his room until now.

Junius put his books down and rolled the globe out of the room, holding the electric cord in his hand so it wouldn't become tangled. When he had it in his own room, he went back for his books and looked around Grandfather's room once, before closing the door firmly behind him. Back in his room, he put his books on his desk and busied himself for a moment finding a place for the globe.

It best be placed over there, he thought, next to the desk and under the window. No. Best pull it away from the window. I will put my desk chair facing the room, behind the globe and under the window when I am not studying. Oh, yea. That tis how I will do it. Let the globe sit, two feet away from that window. And right there is the wall outlet to plug it into.

He plugged in the globe.

Yes! See how it glows!

The soothing, pale-yellow light lit up the pink-and-yellow continents and the blue seas of this spherical model of the Earth. It subdued the harsh angles and corners of his room, touching them with the mystery of twilight. Junius put his desk chair behind the model world and sat down. He placed his hands on the globe, and his palms seemed to gather the light in.

Gret crystal ball, he thought, what does you see? He spun the globe around and found the island chains of the Caribbean. Little dots, spread over the glowing blue ocean like sprinkles of treasure. Miniature pieces of eight. Some islands were not so small. He looked closely, his nose an inch from the dots, and saw that they were outlined in dark blue and shaded in the paler blue of the sea. There were the Greater and Lesser Antilles, the Leeward Islands and the Windward Islands, facing the Caribbean. There the West Indies, with the Sargasso Sea to their backs. The Sargasso Sea was famous for its brown, floating sargasso weed and its calm and mixing ocean currents, so Grandfather had said.

Junius tapped his finger on the independent country of Barbados. He could tap any country he wished and Grandfather's island "lessons" would seep into his brain. In March 1918, the U.S.S. *Cyclops* with an 11,000-ton cargo of Brazillian manganese left Barbados and had not been heard of since. *I remember it well my son,* Grandfather spoke in his memory. *The news of the lost ship spread throughout the island chains. I believed then, at thirteen years old, as I believe now: bloody pirates! Mahn, they did take that ill-fated ship.*

Junius smiled to himself, shook his head. Grandfather held to the fanciful belief that the spirit of pirates had never left the islands.

He tapped the island nation of St. Kitts-Nevis. Grandfather: *Junius son, the sugarcane fields, they flow upward from the island coast, runnin' over the steepness clear to the volcano. I have seen it! Son, you have seen not a thing until you have seen them wavin' stalks of cane bend and part from breezes of the Caribbee Sea. All under the high head of Misery! Oh, yea! That four-thousand-foot volcano all call Mount Misery! On Nevis was your father born, Damius son.*

Junius pondered St. Kitts-Nevis a moment, and then probed the tiny, unknown dot northwest of St. Kitts-Nevis that was Grandfather's island. Once, long ago, known as the Island of Passage, it was now called Snake. *Son. You must see that gret harbor of my Snake. Oh, yea, open and free. Be bounded by low hills, dontcha see. Nobody own that shoreline. The Spanish, they call it* senada honda, *the "deep bay." Hard to describe, my Snake. Tis so hot and dry, the guinea grass grow everywhere. You must take the launch from larger islands to get there over the finest blue water of flyin' fishes you ever see. Snake, no bigger than eight, ten miles length and five miles width. Many coves for boats hiding from the hurricanes. Ha! Hiding from freebooters—they that let others find the loot for them, then they stole it away! The pirate coves!*

"Grandfahtha, you!" Junius murmured, shaking his head again. He felt a deep yearning, a loneliness. These days it was always worse after school, and far worse being so alone.

Junius got up, took his earphones from his desk. They were plugged into his cassette recorder. He pushed down the key to play the tape that he played nearly each day when he came home. Junius seated himself again behind the globe, holding the recorder on his knees, adjusting the headphones over his ears. And the music of Jimi Hendrix seemed to fill his senses, his blood and guts. His world, as he touched the glowing globe.

> *"Stone free*
> *to do what I please,"*

Junius whispered along with the powerful voice.

[33]

> *"Stone free*
> *to ride the breeze.*
> *Stone free*
> *I can't stay.*
> *I got to, gotta get away*
> *right now."*

Hendrix seemed to know and say all the things Junius wanted to know but didn't and needed to say but couldn't. Jimi Hendrix was far different from anyone else in the world, Junius felt. And for him, Hendrix' haunting voice was not dead and would never die.

> *"Will the wind ever remember*
> *the names it has blown in the past?*
> *And with its crutch, its old age and its wisdom*
> *it must know this will be the last.*
> *And the wind cries, Mary."*

Fahtha say he don't make no sense, Jimi Hendrix, Junius thought, through the crying guitars and the driving drumbeat. But he makin' some kind of sense to me, Junius went on. Hendrix know just how like it be feelin' to me. Like, you gotta get away. Like he say, *'Scuse me while I kiss the sky!*

"Oh, mahn," Junius murmured. He got up, Sanyo cassette in hand, and stretched out on the bed on his stomach. His head touched his arm. Not feelin' so good, no, he thought, through the rock-steady music that blasted through the earphones. Feelin' like I can't stand it 'notha minute. Grandfahtha! Tell me a story! Talk to me, Sarrietta. Some*body*! He felt a sob rising.

[34]

He closed his eyes over it; laid his head on the pillow. He turned the music down and started the tape again. Soon, sleep came, suspending him in a place of no hurt.

" *'Scuse me while I kiss the sky!* "

# Four

The winding rim road rose up a cliffside half a mile away across Pelican Cove from Burtie Rawlings' estate. The road was a gradual climb, skirting a grassy, treeless bulge of a hill where island-bred longhorn cattle grazed. Bulls and cows looked like balsa-wood children's toys scattered over the hillside. So old Burtie Rawlings thought as he gazed at them with his naked eye a moment. But quickly, he ducked his head again and went on with his spying through the powerful field glasses.

Burtie sat hidden on a hillock on his own hillside among philodendron tall as men. He wore a U.S. Army-issue camouflage T-shirt and wished now that he'd worn a long-sleeved one. The bloody mimi gnats climbed through the reddish hair of his arms and fed on his sunburnt skin. It was going to rain again. Carefully, he wiped the lenses of the binoculars with a dry piece of tissue he found deep in the binoculars case slung over his shoulder. The air was still; that's why the mimis had attacked. But it would rain without the wind to blow away the languid clouds that slithered one by one over his hills. He'd been soaked twice since he'd come to sit on the hillside. The cliff across the cove hadn't got a drop and he imagined the cattle looking longingly over to where he sat drenched and uncomfortable.

Burtie wore camouflage trousers, too, that bloused over high hiking boots. He wore boots and trousers against attacking termites, scorpions, and the yellow spiders that so terrified Stinking Black Jack.

"The black, stupid fool!" whispered Burtie to the stillness. "Them harmless spiders is but only big and golden, and the least of the poison of this hellhole!"

Burtie lifted the glasses again. He steadied his hands, pressing his elbows into his sides. Spying on the height of the cliff took his attention. Up there sat the square, gray box of a house belonging to Gerard Kostera, the pretender.

"*Oh, yes, I'm the great pretender!*" Burtie murmured a melody from his life thirty-odd years ago when he traveled from the island to America practically every week. But today's the day! he thought. Has to be. It's time!

Gerard Kostera had purchased the gray house from a Snake Islander. And from that high promontory of the cliff Kostera could sight everything coming and going on the bay, and coming in from the Atlantic shores of the island. What Kostera could not see from his house was the Caribbean side of Snake Island. The view was blocked completely by the rolling hills of Burtie's estate.

Burtie smiled to himself, letting what he knew about Kostera roll around in his thoughts. The pretender had come to the Snake and the single town of Lawrence six months ago. Silent, not a tourist and not actually unfriendly, just apart, he had come with no visible means of support. A stocky, strong man, not tall and not short. In no time he became an island explorer, easing into a life of leisure. Bothering no man; spending money for staples in the groceries. Kostera bought scuba equipment. He dived, bringing up fat lobsters and grand grouper for his supper. He swam the many beaches, finding his way to them over the rim road in an army surplus jeep he had purchased for a decent price on the big island and brought to the Snake by car ferry. He fished, hiked, and took nature and sea shots with his camera from the promontory and the high hills and other cliffs. Gerard Kostera was cordial to all; watchful, careful, he was friendly to no one.

That should've been the clue, that there, Burtie thought to himself. He kept his binoculars roving over the house. Each window and the two sides he could see. The jeep was home, if Kostera wasn't. He'd left ten minutes ago.

Ye've got five more minutes to make up yer bloody mind, he told himself. Is today the day or not! He mused on, allowing himself a few minutes more.

Weeks ago, not long after Stinking Jack had returned to the Snake, two men had joined Kostera in the gray house. Their arrival had been a second event for Burtie.

Well, it gets lonely out here, I admit it, he thought.

Pelican Cove, where he lived on the estate, was the least inhabited part of the island, and a good distance from town.

But for the first time, Gerard Kostera's former separation from his fellows made sense in this new situation. The strange men no longer scuba dived, swam, fished, hiked, or took pictures. Gerard shut himself up in the gray house with his companions and no one was the wiser. No one saw or cared, except Burtie Rawlings.

Gives me something to do while Stinking Black Jack is out in the dory.

He had watched Kostera through his field glasses and, sometimes, simply by squinting over there. But with the arrival of the other men, he began watching constantly when alone, from some hidden vantage on his hillside. Steadily watching the stillness above the rim road where nothing moved for hours, for days. The very uneventfulness had intrigued him. At last he caught Kostera and the two men slipping out of the house from the back, where they were in full view of Burtie's estate buildings for only seconds before disappearing over a steep slope.

I spotted them one day, Burtie remembered. Oh, Gawd, what a day that was!

Now Burtie could catch them each day around the same time, leaving the house. Hats pulled far down, shielding their faces. But that first time he'd seen them leave, he had clambered stealthily over the hills, spying on them as they took a circuitous route behind Pelican Cove, skirting close to Burtie's lands, to end up somewhere along the headland, Point Medusa, at the southernmost tip of the island.

By land it was a hard hike to Point Medusa, along a steep path below Burtie's place, along outcroppings that cut off a view of their movements from above. Burtie, scrambling along silently, watching, would lose them there among the outcroppings and the barriers of bush, stubby trees, and mesquite. Any fool knew the short route through Pelican Cove, out to the Bay and around Serpent's Point along the rocky blue Shallows by boat. It was a tricky route, but not all that dangerous.

Just watch out for the rocks of Serpent's Point by the Shallows. Get too close to shore or too far away from it, and you miss the narrow channel through the rocks. And hit the rocks; and lose the boat bottom! he thought now.

Pretty place, Burtie mused, with bright fishes. You

could spot one of the huge turtles now and then.

The Shallows were one of Stinking Jack's favorite fishing spots. Hope the stinking fool caught somethin' big and juicy, Burtie thought.

After the Shallows, glide into Magpie Bay, just a tiny bay, and tie the boat on the craggy shore to a wild palm tree and walk across the inlet. It was a lovely, peaceful thought.

The inlet ain't as much as a quarter mile, Burtie was reminded. But watch out for them stupid longhorns and them wall-eyed horses that roam the place. Gawd! Then parade on through the mesquite. How hot that stuff get in the sun! And them dry trees, the branches, lined all over with them termite trails to the bulgin' nests bigger than beach balls in the tree forks. And there under a coconut palm, down a short space to Medusa Beach. Well, a rocky sand beach ringed with them gorgeous frangipani white flowers and them poison manchineel trees. There, just below Medusa Point. Named from them stingin' medusa jellyfish, too.

So why hadn't Kostera and his men taken a boat? Few people hated boats as Burtie did. Why their tough, concealed walk of a couple of miles each way?

Burtie scrutinized the house on the cliff.

They walk, he thought, because they don't want a soul to see and know where they go.

Ye've had long enough, Burtie. Scoot, mahn, he thought. They're all gone and ye've got yourself plenty time. He slid the case from his shoulder and put his field glasses inside. He left it there, hidden on the hillside. He would find it again easily.

Burtie slid sideways, still crouching, toward the path that led down the hill. He had let the grounds around the path grow high with guinea grass, so that, walking the path, he was hidden still. At the bottom he trudged along truck ruts that led from his property to the rim road. Fences across the road at the bottom of the bulging hills. Fences to keep the cattle restricted. Farmers pretended their cattle got loose; really, they let out the cattle toward hills where the rains fell more often. That was why Burtie kept his property well fenced.

He kept to the shade, opening his gate and closing it behind him. He walked briskly across the road and climbed the easy fence into the cattle area. The cattle were up on the bulge of the cliff hill.

The wretches stay there, with their hind hooves higher than their front, some devil herd, Burtie thought. Though he perspired, he was glad to be moving, glad he had taken action at last.

He skirted along the bottom of the hill that took him below and slightly to the right of the gray cliff house. There it was a much easier climb up, and a much more secluded one, than taking the rim road would have been. By the manner in which the ground was tramped muddy, he realized his route up was exactly the one Kostera and his companions took down.

Burtie emptied his mind of fear. He kept caution with him, but he wasn't afraid. He had enough Planter's

Punch in him to keep him in a steady, brave mood. He pulled on worn work gloves. His mind emptied of everything save the energy it took him to climb. Before he knew it, he was at the back of the house, breathing deeply, but not hard. He had his plastic strips in his hand and a flat piece of metal if the strips didn't work. Two old credit cards of slightly different widths. He slid the thinnest in and it was just right. He had counted on the Kostera bunch thinking they had all the locals bamboozled. He was positive that by his own antics they thought him nothing more than a broken-down, cursing drunk.

Burtie smiled. There were no new locks on the rear door. The strip did its work and there was a click as he turned the door handle. The door swung free.

I'm in! Gawd!

Large, shadowy rooms. Heat held in by gray louvers over screened windows. The sun burned down on the unshaded house. He would have died if he had found a soul sitting in the chair across from him that faced the room. It was the single cushioned wicker chair in the entire rear kitchen that was as large as a parlor room. Chairs at the table were L.L. Bean captain's chairs, worth over fifty dollars apiece. A high price for chairs like the kind Burtie had owned, with oak frames, that had cost him no more than eighteen dollars apiece fifteen years ago. He'd got rid of them at a good price, too. These Kostera chairs had canvas fabric. His mind seemed to be picking up every stupid detail.

Burtie went through the whole one-story house. He found Kostera's scuba and swimming equipment in one small back room. In another room he found two bunks, open satchels. A closet with expensive sailing clothes, well worn. The bunk room had to be the place where the two new men stayed. But Burtie knew that any find would be close in to where Kostera spent most of his time. The front parlor room had been divided by two-by-fours into sitting room and bedroom. Burtie looked over the bedroom first. It would be Gerard Kostera's.

He touched objects with his gloved hands only when he had to. Most of the time he used the credit cards, raising the edges of papers here and there with them and the metal piece.

There was a desk, the top covered with a sheet of plywood and weighted down with a cement block. Carefully, Burtie lifted the block and set it on the floor. He just as carefully lifted the plywood and set it aside.

"Bingo! What nice fellows we have here," Burtie whispered. The desk was covered with goodies, a regular factory for phony ID papers. He'd found what he was looking for. No, not exactly. He hadn't known what he was looking for. He simply knew that Kostera was up to something in the direction of Burtie's own lands, and that made Burtie very nervous and, also, envious.

Whatever the pie, should Kostera get it all? Why shouldn't I get a piece of it? Burtie thought.

Glancing around, he stooped to look under the bed, and discovered a whole kit and caboodle for altering passports. He found three passports under the bed pillow.

Jesus! Did *he* think he was safe!

Two passports belonging to Ghennady Kotkind and one belonging to Gerard Kostera. Gerard Kostera's heavy-featured face showed on all three passports.

Burtie whistled softly. The Kostera passport made Gerard British. The Kotkind ones showed him as American and Australian, respectively.

Burtie smiled. He had seen enough. But he noticed a small artist's paintbox in a corner. He opened it to discover assorted drivers' licenses in five different names. And Social Security card forgeries. Wonderful.

Get out, he thought. But I need to know where they come from really. What does it matter? But the passports are lies. Kotkind/Kostera is neither British, American, or Australian. How so? Burtie had no clear answer to the question. He simply knew all the passports would be phony. He recognized the undercover kind, the way he knew himself in his thieving heart as a scheming, part-criminal, part-heathen son of an island planter.

"If ye hid well, ye might get a good look at them when they come back," he whispered. Get out!

It kept nagging him—get out! Even though the men wouldn't be back so soon, he didn't think.

He would get out. But first he replaced everything

the way it had been. Plywood board, cement block, passports, pillow. Everything. He glanced all around and went out through the rooms to the back, a thin specter in the shadowy place.

He was on the far side of the house, away from his property, his view blocked by hills. He did not so much hear them coming back. His sixth sense was working. And he reacted, cringing smaller, before he heard the men.

Gawd! Had they seen him leave the house? Not likely!

There was nowhere to hide save a thick stand of mesquite about halfway down the hillside. No flat place, no boulders.

Oh, my Gawd! Burtie dove for the mesquite. He plunged and rolled at once, keeping quiet and trying to shield himself from the two-inch mesquite thorns. It was no use. He grabbed blindly. He held to the mesquite where his hands landed. Good thing he wore gloves, but they couldn't save him. He had to crawl deeper into the stuff, gritting his teeth. He was terrified of screaming and he swore he wouldn't.

The men were near. The way took them from his right, climbing to his left, above him.

Goodness. Goodness. Gawd!

But he managed to hold on, to open his eyes and watch. The men were cautious, looking this way and that. One of them seemed to look right at Burtie without recognition. Desperately, Burtie shut his eyes, as if by closing them he could make himself disappear.

He didn't see me. He didn't miss a single step as he looked!

Their hats low over their faces as they passed on out of sight. Funny kind of angled hats. Not oval at all, but having three sides with the softly rolled point of one side down low in the front. The last man, the one who had looked down toward Burtie, had an evil-looking unsheathed machete tied to his belt. He wore creaseless trousers bloused over high boots. Mean-looking face, what Burtie had seen of it. Fierce eyes under thick brows.

Burtie had lain where he was too long. Ants came swiftly out of the mesquite, marching down his shoulder, getting under his T-shirt at the neck. He nearly screeched in agony from their burning bites but held himself in. At last he scrambled around getting out of there. The bites turned into nasty welts before he could slap the ants off and was back to safety. The welts itched painfully.

Once back on his own land Burtie picked up his binoculars case, then went into the bathroom to find some antiseptic for his left hand. The thorns had fairly torn up his palm. Then he bandaged the whole thing. All he had was tape. It would give him the devil when he tried to remove it in a few days. Last, he cleansed the ant welts, red trails afire across his chest and shoulders.

He was back outside again, heading down his hillside and thinking, Safe! Safe! My own land and never a soul better trespass! He stayed low, for Kostera was home, although no one would know from looking at the house. It looked empty, as it had been before.

Who are they and what are they after? Burtie wondered. I got me a good idea. If I had a swell-looking schooner and I was travelin' by night and doin' bad-such by day, I know where I'd heave to! Sure, a blasted back island with hardly a population to call decent. And that what it had that was free and white bein' half baked and sodden with rum. Ha!

He glanced up to see Stinking Black Jack himself heading in. Pausing, Burtie stared into the distance.

Know it's you, you old, stinking fogey! He recognized the dory and Stinking Black Jack as a dark obstacle trailing a foaming wake on the expanse of the bay. The white arrow wake guided the eye toward the deep, blue Atlantic spreading across the entire north beyond island hills. Impossible for Burtie to tell where ocean ended and sky began. But the shadow point of man and boat, the white arrow and the turquoise-and-blue sweep, made a striking picture for Burtie from his hillside. A sign that he was well and secure from a ragged world on his own free land. Thinking, *My land!* Indeed, it was his land, although he was sick to death of it.

I'd ruther be anywhere else! he raged inside. Just a little stash is all I need.

Burtie went on down to shore. He was feeling proud of himself and he gave one last glance to the Kostera house. I'm a danged smart fellow, if I do say so.

Investigator Burtie Rawlings, he was!

# Five

Junius' father came home from work about the same time each night. In the winter it was always dark when he came home. And dark in the morning when he went to work.

Dark for my father, dark, Junius thought. I don't mind him dark.

He smiled. Daddy so dark island mahn, it tis shown right away that he not an American black mahn. He is different. Terribly slender. Even slim North American black mahn have more muscle. He have the muscle, my dad do, but you can't see them, dontcha know, 'cause the way he built, they does not show. Long, muscles stretch lengthways. He walkin', long strides, slowly like somebody done slow down the life of the mahn. The picture of him, slow motion, suit jacket flapping away. Funny so, mahn, my fahtha. Like he running in his walking. Little mustache. Hair skinhead short. He a smart fahtha, so they say. But he don't like to hurry or push himself too fast. He happy the way it tis. I don't mind the way it tis. Muhtha happy, too. We got plenty. I like eatin' my supper every night, sem way, sem table, sem conversation. It don't bore me. But I wish for Grand*fahtha*. That has changed and made me not so happy now. Every night, sleeping, I see his face, old mahn. Worry over him, his face lookin' like it ready to call me for somethin' special. I don't like the dreamin' like that. I have me a bellyful of dreamin' bad. Somethin' not straight with Grandfahtha. Wish he would write me.

Another weekend comin' up soon. This, Thursday. Tomorrow, Friday.

Junius sighed. Maybe he would go to the basketball game, and after, the dance. Maybe he would go see another movie. Maybe there would be something interesting on cable. But it would be better to get out of the house. Could he chance the whole world seeing him going to the movies with his mother and father again? If he went to the dance, he would go alone. He knew he would.

Grandfahtha haven't written in so long. Maybe tomorrow.

Junius had done all his homework. They were piling on the work toward the holidays coming in a few weeks. Some teachers planned even to give homework over the holidays. It was hard now even for Junius to keep up. English, Spanish. So much social studies, time lines. He was beginning to hate school, sounding like many of the students before the holidays. He was hating some of the teachers. Got it in his head, sometimes, that they didn't like teenagers much. But still, he was managing, with all the work of studying and learning. He came home right after school now. At his corner he left the kids walking toward downtown. He would not go through it again, like the last time, Monday, he had followed them downtown and found himself sitting by himself at the counter, just forgotten by all of them, his classmates. He wouldn't chance being left out another time.

He closed his English book. And stood, stretching. He got up, left his room. From the hall he could hear his mother in the kitchen, preparing supper.

I will go help her, he thought. Somethin' to do and make her happy, too. She like me comin' in, talkin' to her about my day.

Junius heard a car stop. He was in the hall that led from the living room and left turned past his bedroom going toward the kitchen. He went to the living room and the front door. He looked out the window and was shocked by what he saw. A gray car at the curb, waiting. And Sarrietta Dobbs coming up on his front porch.

Sarrietta Dobbs, most beautiful young woman! The last person he hoped ever to see coming his way. In a trance, he opened the door and peered out into the cold. It felt like a curtain he couldn't quite see through.

"Tis a dream," he said, hardly realizing he had spoken out loud. "But why, if I be dreamin', my eyes wide open? Why I'm feeling the cold in my face if I be dreamin'?"

Sarrietta Dobbs giggled. "I heard that!" she said lightly. She stood before him in a rush of perfumed air that made his head spin. "Junius? Hi! I tried to call you, but they said your phone is out of order. Can I come in? Are you busy? If you're not, I'll tell Mama to go ahead on."

"Tell Mama to go ahead on," he whispered. "Tell Mama, do."

Sarrietta laughed. "Junius, you're so funny!" she said. She waved her mother on; the big car slid easily away from the curb.

"Sweet Sarrietta have to stay here foreveh," Junius said softly.

"How come?" she said playfully.

"Mama can't call you home if my phone does be out of order!" he said.

That made her giggle again. "Are you going to let me in? Oh! I forgot to say why I'm here."

"You here because you cahn't stay away from Junius Rawlings."

"Junius! I need help with my G-O. Can you help me?"

G-O was what the students called geometry. The subject seemed to be endlessly perplexing to them, and those in the class were mostly juniors. Sarrietta was in some of his classes. He had simply assumed that she was older than him. But now he began to suspect that she was his age and in an accelerated program just like he was. And having trouble, now.

He put his arms around her, lifting her up the one step from the porch into the house. He felt her stiffen. When he set her down, she pushed at him. "Don't *do* that!" she said. She swung her armful of books at him. "What right do you have to do that!"

"But you let Plas do that," he said. "He putting both his arms around you."

"I didn't *let* him. I don't," she said. "He does it and I don't *like* it."

Junius let his arms drop to his sides. "I thought . . ." he began, embarrassed.

"No!" she said. "I don't like it. And boys who don't realize that aren't really my friends."

He stared at her. "And you tellin' me . . ." he said.

"Junius, you're not like the other guys," she finished for him. "You are different. I mean, I don't mean that in a bad way. Just don't try to act like them. Because you can't. I mean, you are *nice*," Sarrietta said. He noticed that it seemed hard for her to say that. Could it be that she was as shy as he, he wondered.

"Here, let's not be standing in this open door," he said, and quickly shut the door behind them. They were in the hall now. He motioned her along but she didn't move.

"Is your mother at home?" Sarrietta asked. Suddenly she looked frightened, as though the thought had just occurred to her. "I was supposed to ask that, first." He knew she wouldn't stay if his mother was not at home.

So beautiful! he thought. Little and sweet. I won't ever hurt you. Never try to put my arm around you, you don't want me to. Just be here with you, enough for Junius son!

"Think my mama gettin' ready to make supper. Come," he said. And she followed him down the hall that left turned to the kitchen. There they found his mother.

"Muhtha," Junius said, "Sarrietta Dobbs is here. She couldn't get us on the phone. It seem to be out of order."

"Really?" said his mother. "Hello, Sarrietta. It's so nice to see you."

"Hello, Mrs. Rawlings," Sarrietta said.

Mrs. Rawlings smiled and picked up the phone on the wall, listening a moment. "It sounds dead, all right," she said. "No dial tone. Just static. I'll go next door and call. . . ." She looked enquiringly at Junius.

"Sarrietta and I planning to study some geometry," he said.

"I'm having problems with it," Sarrietta explained. "Junius knows everything about math."

"We have a pretty humongous test comin' up soon," he said. He glanced shyly at Sarrietta. She looked down at her feet, holding her books tightly to her.

Again his mother looked on approvingly.

"Muhtha, can Sarrietta stay for supper?"

"Oh, I couldn't!" Sarrietta said.

"Well, you are welcome to," said Mrs. Rawlings. "We're just having macaroni and cheese tonight."

"My favorite," Junius said. He never took his eyes away from Sarrietta. "Do stay," he said. "That way we can be studying all the way to supper and again after. Maybe we take supper right in my room."

"Yes, you can do that," his mother said.

"It's okay," Sarrietta said. Junius knew that in the parlance of the students, that meant that she had no objection to staying.

"Well, you're welcome to stay," his mother said.

"That's okay," Sarrietta said. And Junius smiled.

Mrs. Rawlings went out, grabbing her coat and scarf first, to use the neighbors' phone.

Junius and Sarrietta stood there in the kitchen. "Tis somethin'!" he said. "The phones go out for no reason. A big storm come and all the lights go out, too."

"That's a small town for you," she said. "Shaky civilization." She giggled.

"You rather be in a city?" he asked her.

"Sometimes, when the phone goes out, and the lights."

"Yeah," he said. "I agree. But other times I like it all right."

"Yeah, me too," she said. "But I won't be able to stay for supper if I can't call my mother and tell her."

Kitchen no place to stand and talk, he thought. "If

our phone not fixed, then we just use Mr. Kendall's next door, okay?" he said.

She nodded.

"Come on. We best get started." He led her back up the hall to his room.

"This is a nice room," she said, once they were inside. He was careful to leave the door wide open.

"Thank you," Junius said. "I'll hang your coat up in the closet. Just put your books there on the desk." When she sat down primly at his desk, turned sideways toward the room, he quickly took his book out and a notebook. Found a pencil.

She was looking at everything, and Junius realized that this was the first time he had ever had another teenager in his room. He sat down on his bed, watching her.

She smiled suddenly, turning to look at him shyly. She looked pleased to be where she was. That made him happy.

"I like that globe over there," she said. "I've only seen one that large in the library. It must come in handy."

Memories of Grandfather Jackabo came unbidden. "It will light up, once you plug it in," he said. "Show you later."

They began to study. He asked her to pull her chair closer to him, so he could show her. When she was right next to him, he began to ask her questions.

"What's the problem for you?" he said.

"All of it, I guess. I can't seem to get it through my thick skull. All those proofs!"

"What did you get on the last test?" he asked.

"A D!" she said. "I tore it up."

"Should have kept it," he said gently. "We could work from it. But here." He took out his own test from his geometry folder. "I got minus one off for not gettin' my altitude lines crossed at the right place. See?"

"But you got a ninety-nine," she said. "You get fantastic grades."

"It's concentration," he told her. "It's knowing the basic rules and how to think about them, that's all it tis."

"Well," she said softly.

It was always difficult teaching the intelligent poor student, he knew. For it embarrassed them not to do well. He often tutored students. Sarrietta would have found that out, and that was why she had come for help. Junius knew she hadn't come because of himself. It was a beginning, though, between them, he thought.

"All right," he said. "Let us take the question of altitude on the test. Problem five. Define 'altitude.' Draw a triangle and all its altitudes. Do it," he told her.

"An equilateral triangle?" she asked.

"Yes. Fine. Do it," he told her.

She drew the triangle with three equal sides.

"Now what?" he said.

"I . . . don't know," she answered.

"What is altitude? Do you know what it tis?"

"Yes," she said.

"Show me."

She drew a line from the point where two of the sides met to the opposing side.

"Now say what you just did in words."

She thought a moment and shook her head.

"Say it like this," he said. " 'Altitude. The perpendicular distance from a vertex to a side.' Say it."

She said it perfectly.

"Write it down." She did.

"I'm not sure what vertex means," she said, keeping her eyes on her notebook.

"Can you show me where it tis?" he asked. She showed him.

"Then vertex is the point of intersection of two sides, yes?"

She nodded.

"Say it," he said.

She did.

"Now write it." She wrote it.

"So then, this must always be the process for you," he said. "You picture how to do somethin'. You do it, if you can. You say what you have done in words. And write it down. The written words show you the truth or the proof of what you have done."

"You make it sound so simple," she said. She sighed.

"It tis not quite simple," he said. "It takes work. But

you will find every bit of it in the book. You must read the instructions for the problems given. Most students get confused because they try to do the problems first before reading about them."

"I do that," she said. "I get bored reading all those examples."

"Well, you must do it from now on," he said. "You come by as often as you can for a couple of hours, and you'll learn how the G-O is thought about." He smiled at her.

She was looking at him in a new light, he thought, as though she were seeing him in a new set, a different circumstance. And for the rest of the studying, he was careful to stay on the subject of geometry. Later, the phone got fixed and they called her mother and she was allowed to stay for supper.

A little before suppertime, they filled their plates and ate in Junius' room at little tables his mother provided. They had a sweet time, too. He allowed himself to flirt outrageously, feeling devilish.

His father came home.

Junius' first impulse was to shout, "Fahtha! Come meet Sarrietta Dobbs! We been studyin', see?" But he didn't know. He would have liked to kid with his father, putting the island accent on heavily. But his father rarely kidded. There was something ever polite and fixed between the two of them. Junius knew that his father cared for him. But there was always a boundary between. There was never the simple give and take, the easy affection that existed between Junius and Grandfather Jackabo.

He doesn't like to hear about the islands or to hear me speak like an island mahn, Junius thought.

"I left the islands long ago for good," he had told Junius more than once. But there would be a troubled, longing look in his eyes as he said it.

At last Junius called, "Fahtha? There is somebody here I would like you to meet." He stiffened, sat up straighter. Sensing his tension, Sarrietta Dobbs took a deep breath and stared at the doorway. Everybody knew about Junius' father, and how aloof he was.

Mr. Rawlings came to stand there; he did not enter the room. He was very tall, a slim and dark man. He bowed courteously, then looked inquiringly at Junius.

"Good evening, Fahtha," Junius said.

"Good evening, Junius, how are you?" said his father.

"I am fine, Fahtha," Junius said. "Fahtha, this is Sarrietta Dobbs. Sarrietta, this is my fahtha, Mr. Rawlings." There, Junius thought. I did that pretty well.

"Good evening, Sarrietta," Mr. Rawlings said. "I am pleased to meet you."

"Hi," she said, hardly above a whisper.

"I know your father," Mr. Rawlings said.

She looked up, then hurriedly down. "Oh, yes," she said.

Quickly, Junius said, "We have been studyin' geometry."

Mr. Rawlings looked at Sarrietta in his reserved, unsmiling way.

"I . . . I have trouble with it," she managed. "He's . . . Junius is tutoring me."

Mr. Rawlings nodded. "It's good to get at the trouble right away," he said. He smiled and added, "Excuse me, won't you?" and turned away. Junius knew he would now have his supper in the kitchen with Junius' mother.

"Whew!" Sarrietta said. "I don't think he likes me here."

"It's not that," Junius said. "He just not too comfortable with people. He wants to be like everybody, American. He manages to talk just like everybody, but he's not like everybody inside, and it shows on the outside. But he don't know that."

She smiled at Junius and nodded. "You don't get along with him?"

"Oh, we get along. I get along with him, long as I don't talk about the islands."

They set aside the small tables holding their empty supper plates, and Junius showed Sarrietta Grandfather's globe. He stood above her, while she sat there at the globe. Her hands were poised over its light. She had her index finger on Grandfather's tiny dot of an island. Looking around at Junius, she rested her head lightly against his arm. He looked down into her lovely eyes. He had the urge to take her by the shoulders in a gentle caress. But he did not. He touched her hair ever so lightly. It made her smile shyly down at the globe again. He did not let his hand linger. But he could tell she did not mind his touch. He could tell she liked him.

# Six

Burtie waited on the sagging planks of the Rawlings family dock. He had grabbed up an old *paja* from the cement steps above the dock. It was the straw hat with a low crown, to keep the sun off his face. His face looked burnt raw, although half of the effect was his complexion. He'd rolled his pant legs and taken off his boots and socks to dangle his bare feet above the waterline. Why he needed his pant legs rolled when he kept his feet dry was a mystery. He tried to make it appear he'd been sitting there perhaps for hours, for Stinking Jack's benefit as well as Kostera's, staring at the deep and listening to its lapping at the dock pilings.

Not unusual for islanders, to sit in the dock breezes during the stifling heat hours of the late afternoon. Maybe Stinking Black Jack would see through him. Burtie didn't care as long as dirty Jack didn't question him.

Old heathen Burtie, as Jackabo called him, despised

all boating piers. He didn't care that the Rawlings dock was in disrepair and would slowly slide into the sea someday. He simply didn't intend to give Black Jack the pleasure of knocking it down. Burtie shunned the sea, although as a lad he had cared for it a bit. But these days he pretended he'd rather walk the four miles into town instead of taking the short trip by boat up the bay to the town wharf. Truth was, he didn't want to leave his hillside where he could spy. And no one need know that but him.

Water was good for looking at and into, and for fishing, he thought tiredly. He tolerated it enough to sit in a boat and troll for fish. But now he had Stinking Black Jack, and he needn't get in the bloody bobbing dory at all. Sea was good for the scenery of it, for the way it set off the bulging brown-and-green hills and the burning cliffs just so, and for little else.

Burtie got painfully to his feet. Stinking Jack was making his turn around Pelican Cove and heading in. Being there on the dock to help meant that Burtie could stop the son of a black fool from coming in too fast, cutting the engine too late and ramming the dock. Not that he cared about the dock. But so far, Stinking Jack took care and came in slow. Burtie was on one knee, his good hand held out to the boat by the time Stinking Black Jack cut the motor and nosed the dory smoothly home. He helped Black Jack by taking hold of the bow before it could hit the dock, and then holding it steady while Stinking Jack tied up to a cleat.

The two enemies spoke not a word. They needed no words to dock a boat, to complete this necessary ritual of island life. Burtie knew he must look dusty atop his sweat. He was dusty from his time of "investigating"—he hoped Black Jack would think he had been lazing on the hillside. The Rawlings Estate, known by black islanders as Eh-tah Raw*leen*, was the broad back of a narrow headland.

Burtie could smell the fresh sea surrounding Black Jack. But he would not look at the skinny black fool. He waited, sitting patiently again, as Jackabo stepped up onto the dory's prow and kicked off his sandals.

Stinking Black Jack took off his filthy shift of monk's cloth, folding it neatly. He let it drop down on the seat. He removed the knife he always wore. Then, balancing, he walked the cross seats to the other end. Wheezing like an old goat, Burtie thought. Standing on a side seat next to the motor, dirty Jack dived out toward deeper water. Still, the depth was shallow so near the shore, and his leap out was much too short. It was feeble, was Burtie's opinion. But Stinking Jack wasn't aware of this. He was so forgetful, he did not remember he was an old mahn! One day he would dive and his head would get stuck in the muddy bottom. His big feet and skinny legs would tangle among the mangrove roots. The thought made Burtie grin.

Here we are, the exact same age, Burtie thought. Grown up on this very same land.

"Yer muhtha work for mine!" Burtie hollered, suddenly. But Jackabo missed it, being still under water.

Barely remember what she look like, Burtie thought, about Black Jack's mother. Skinny woman, purple lips, always teaching Black Jack things, history—what for? He only a black. Then they leave the islands. And come back, and leave again.

Now he and I old. Why cannot I recall each passing day? Such a long time growin' old! And so suddenly old.

But the black, Burtie thought, he have mostly no mind now. And I—I mind too much, heh! One day Black Jack be too old to go into town to cash his government check. I'll go for him and I'll take of it what I want!

Taking money from a black fool was dumb luck compared to what else seemed to be going on. Old Burtie knew the foul taste of danger. Still, he was not entirely certain what the extent of it was. His uneasiness had started from a growing awareness of something out of place. It had progressed to the general observation of an oddity. Finally, Burtie had a definite suspicion. And after the proof of today, he knew he would be on edge most of the time. It made him need to drink more Planter's Punch. He couldn't wait to get home. And sitting down in the sun of the dock, careful of his hand, too, made him feel giddy.

Sourly, stealthily, Burtie watched Stinking Jack. No longer did he fear the fool drowning in the sea as he had at first, when Black Jack had come back.

"Stay away from the water, fool, ye don't know how to swim it," he had told dirty Jack. But Black Jack merely had shown his pink gums and very white, perfect false teeth. Burtie wished he had a son to fix him up with good teeth like that.

They must've costed a thousand dollars, Burtie thought. Black Jack say they costed *two* thousand dollars, but Burtie knew that was a lie. All he had was an ex-wife somewhere in south Florida, and he hoped never to lay eyes on her again. It was because the few teeth he had left were so poor that he drank much more than he ate. But surely he could do with a good son like Stinking Jack's.

Burtie recalled that as a child, Black Jack had thrashed his way through the swells along the reefs, holding on to the slimy rocks, cutting his hands on the coral. Screaming all day for Burtie to wait for him, or come to his rescue. Burtie thought, And to think I was the white and he the black. And he callin' for me to "rescure" *him*.

Now, in his old age, old Stinking Black Jack had forgotten he couldn't swim. He swam and he dived like a porpoise, the fool.

The Devil take him, thought Burtie. No, the Devil likely have much better sense than that!

Burtie waited while Black Jack had his swim, squinting away across Pelican Cove to the rim road. It was a thrill for him now to see that house and to know he had been there and gone, and none up there the wiser.

But there was no point in trying to make Stinking Black Jack move along out of the sea before he was ready. The fish dirty Jack had caught for their supper, Burtie decided, would have to wait a little longer.

Stinking Black Jack lay on his back in the water like he was asleep in his filthy bed.

Gawd! Burtie thought. Ye think he remembers where he's rottin' at? Burtie decided to leave dirty Jack alone for another minute. But Stinking Black Jack was pulling himself up on the boat. The suddenness of his move startled Burtie. He watched the black taking time, struggling to climb back in the dory. Such a climb wasn't easy. Absently, Burtie hopped down onto the prow, to make the boat sit lower in the water. It made it easier for Black Jack to pull himself in.

Grandfather Jackabo managed to get up, with a hand from Burtie. He gathered his clothing to sit on the dock a moment.

"Ye stayed in too long, stinking fool," Burtie said, half under his breath.

"Oh, hush up, you heathen skunk!" said Jackabo crossly. He was tired now and there was still the hill to climb up to the rooms. Wearily, he glanced around at the sun-baked hillside and put on his cloak and sandals. Put on the knife he always wore.

Grandfather Jackabo gathered his old bones and got up slowly from the dock. He walked away toward the path that led halfway across the base of the hill before going up.

"Huh?" said Burtie. "Hey, whoa, ye son of a . . . Where ye think yer off to without that fish bucket?"

"Carry it yourself," said Jackabo. "And bring that fire pot with you. I et all up the fungi—hee, hee!"

"Yer dang fungi was rotted to begin with. It tasted foul from the start!" Burtie yelled after him. "Stop, you, and carry these fishes!" Burtie was down in the boat now. He slung the fungi pot up his arm above the elbow.

Grandfather Jackabo had stopped in his tracks. Slowly he turned around toward Burtie. He looked shocked, with his mouth shaped in a gaping O.

Burtie peered into the fish bucket. "Why, it's empty. Where're the fishes!" he hollered. "Ye caught no fishes, ye black devil!"

Grandfather Jackabo looked confused. He commenced to tremble, clutching one hand with the other. In the silence of the day, Burtie could hear what he said quite plainly, although Black Jack spoke softly. "I . . . I forget all about it. . . . I . . . Oh, darn me, I . . . forget to go fishin'. . . ."

"You fool!" cried Burtie. But he was silenced when, suddenly, Jackabo seemed to falter there and fell to one knee.

Burtie stood still, but only for a moment. Quickly, he was out of the boat and up on the dock. He moved well for his age, lacking any disease of the joints. He never took his eyes off Black Jack, not even when he bent down to pick up his old enemy's bamboo staff from the dockside, that Stinking Jack had used to get down the hill at the start of the day. Burtie took it over to him. Jack had got the one knee off the ground again.

"I'm winded," Jackabo said, weakly, by way of explanation. Sweat poured from his forehead.

"Aye, ye think you're a lad of twenty, that's yer trouble," Burtie said gruffly. He took Black Jack under the arms and stood him on his feet. He gave over the staff, wrapping Jack's fingers around the wood. "There," he said. "Lean on that. I'll hold yer other arm." He pushed the fungi pot up and around behind his shoulder so he could manuever better.

"No need. No need," Grandfather Jackabo was saying. But Burtie held him and Black Jack did not resist.

"It was that danged hot sun," Grandfather whispered as they made their way. He stumbled and Burtie held him firmly.

"Aye, the sun," Burtie said, grimly. "Don't try to talk. Save the strength."

"I ain't weak!" Grandfather Jackabo said. "It was the rain, comin' on me so sudden, like. Did I say how it soaked me through, filled me mouth up?"

"Aye, and hush up now, mahn. We got a hill to go." The arm is just bone! Burtie thought, shocked by the feel of Black Jack's weak body. He's decayin'. Weakening. Dyin' old!

[71]

"If it hadn'ta rained down, I woulda remembered the fishin', dontcha see?"

"I know that, ye stinking wreck," said Burtie. "Now will ye stop with yer chewin' off my ear?"

"Huh!" Jackabo murmured. "Gawd, the hill grows higher!" They were at the foot of it. It went straight up, tall guinea grass on either side of the path. Rock and a thin layer of dirt over the rock. Steps had been cut into the rock long ago. Now they were worn smooth, nothing more than shallow impressions in the poor soil.

"What'll we eat, then?" Grandfather thought to ask.

"Whatdya think, mahn? I got Spam. I got that wretched gray stuff they call hamburger in the shops of Lawrence. Ye want that?"

"Smother him in the onion and canned tomato, and Spanish red pepper."

"If I got it, I will do that," Burtie said. "Just remember, yer to blame for our starvation."

"Sorrow, pity me," Old Jackabo murmured. He turned toward Burtie and tripped. Burtie caught him with careful indifference, shoved him vertical again.

"I'll boost ye, get going," Burtie said. "I might even carry ye, ye weightless sad sack."

"Huh!" was all Grandfather could manage. They struggled up the hillside. Grandfather Jackabo leaned heavily on his staff. Closed his eyes more than once. His wheezing breath filled the air.

"He's catching the asthma, I know it! Or the hay fever," Burtie told himself. "It's that burstin', fillin' scent of the grasses after a rain. It makes even my nose itch and twitch."

Burtie pushed Grandfather Jackabo. He lifted him by the arms, shoved him now and then from behind. He cursed old age under his breath. And thought: Stinking Black Jack is goin' over, it's bound to come. And I will be in charge of buryin' the devil! Won't tell a soul, neither. Just him and me, even when he be a mahn six feet under. And then this hillside will march higher for old Burtie, I'll wager.

The smothering heat filled Burtie's nostrils. Sweat swam down his sides and back. His injured hand ached. The ant welts stung badly.

And who will boost me up? he thought, about the hillside. The very idea seemed to shimmer in a hellish sun-scorched heat. And who will pick up the bleached bones of me for decent burial after I fall down the last long time?

The notion of himself dying and growing cold, stiffening, on the sweltering hillside was horrid enough to make old Burtie grin, like the condemned scoundrel he was. He laughed heartily all the way up the hill until he was panting painfully, himself. The Planter's Punch he'd consumed during the day had already made cotton candy of his brain.

# *Seven*

Well, I sure have been *dwellin'*, Grandfahtha, Junius thought. His mother had said just the other day that he should dwell on something other than Grandfather.

But I haven't forgotten you one bit, Grandfahtha, he thought. I'll write him that, too.

Junius was home. He had spoken a greeting to his mother and made small talk—*How was school, Junius? School was fine, Muhtha. How did the Spanish test go? Got an A minus. The woman take off two points for a single accent mark I forget. Tough lady*—that sort of thing. He had a long drink of orange juice in the kitchen, and thought to ask as he did each day whether there was a letter yet from Grandfather. There was! His mother handed it over. A big, fat letter, postmarked November 25th.

"You see how long it take to get here?" he said, excitedly to his mother. "Why it have to take so long!"

he complained. "Does not the Snake belong to these gret United States?"

"You know the islands are a long way away," his mother told him. "Any letter has to get to the big island by ferry or little plane, and then from there it's flown to some distribution point, I would guess, here in the U.S. And we don't know how long it takes Grandfather Jackabo to find his envelopes and find his stamps and put the address on and mail the letter."

Junius agreed there was a lot he didn't know. Looking at the letter, he saw dirt marks and what he took to be perspiration, or seawater marks.

"Next time, I will ask him everything about it," Junius said. He left his mother to go read the letter in private in his room. The letter was addressed to him and his father and mother. Mr. Junius Rawlings first. Then Mr. and Mrs. D. Rawlings.

And now he was in his room, straightening the already neat area before he settled down to read the letter. Sarrietta Dobbs would be coming over. He sure was dwelling on Sarrietta Dobbs! Wednesday and she'd been coming over to study each day. Junius didn't think about why or how anymore, for fear thinking would make it become unreal and Sarrietta Dobbs just something beautiful and make-believe to comfort himself.

She waited for him after the last class at school. "Will you be comin' over today, Sarrietta?" he asked her. The last two days he had asked this question. And she had nodded each time. "I'll be over, Hey-mahn. . . ." And shyly, "Junius, I mean, same time. You wait for me, now, before you start studying the G-O."

And all the other students, so quick to notice. The guys like Plas and Slam, saying, "Look! Look at Junie-mahn and Shoog! Call HBO! Look at Junie-mahn and Shoog! Ooh, that is *deep*, man! Wish I was him, shoot."

It had embarrassed Junius so. And he had been afraid that Sarrietta would run away from him. But she didn't get angry at him. She ignored the guys. She stuck her nose up and went on about her business.

Sarrietta Dobbs should know that Junius Rawlings will wait for her, on her, or any other kind of wait she want, Junius was thinking.

He turned on Grandfather Jackabo's globe in preparation for reading the letter. He pulled the chair over a bit from the globe so he could cross his long legs and sit comfortably. Junius could barely contain his excitement. A flood of memories came back to him, all the good times with Grandfather. He forced himself to take his time, take a deep breath. Then he spun the globe around until he found the Caribbean islands and the little island dot that was the Snake. Somehow, looking down on the glowing dot put him closer to Grandfather's island home. He imagined he could hear the sea. That Grandfather was looking up and seeing a light glowing in the sky that he couldn't explain. The light would be Junius' own eyes shining on Grand-father.

"*'Scuse me while I kiss the sky!*"

Carefully, he opened the letter. Ah! He imagined a faint whiff of salt air, and the scent of spices. And just as he had hoped, there was another seashell inside, wrapped in one half of a lunch napkin. Carefully, Junius opened the napkin. The seashell, white, this time, was broken into tiny pieces.

Why must it break? he thought. He touched the pieces tenderly with the tips of his fingers. How so sad! The shells were always smashed. Never were they delivered to Junius in one piece, as Grandfather Jackabo would have wished.

Grandfather loved to send small shells to Junius. And when Junius wrote him back, he was careful not to reveal the fate of the shells through the U.S. mail.

This letter was a long one, in Grandfather's tiny hand. He had told Junius once that it would not bother him to write pages and pages. But Junius guessed it did bother Grandfather.

Grandfather Jackabo used a kind of shorthand, run-ning words and sentences together, changing the spell-ings of words. It was his own special way of showing all that he was thinking.

Junius felt a lump in his throat. A longing. He swal-lowed hard. Glanced at his watch. He had forty-five minutes or so, before Sarrietta would arrive.

The letter was four pages long, written on tablet paper. The paper was yellow, with blue lines and wide spaces between the lines. Grandfather wrote at least two rows of words in each wide space.

Good, oh, good, thought Junius. He is writing me a lot. This, Junius read:

Junius son! Damius my son my own boy! Daughterinlaw Jaylene!

Oh, are mine you really there! All of you over so far, I cannot think on it. It make me so sick to my heart to think how Junius son over far and you all far so far. But this is home, I miss you! I don't miss there. Cold. Junius you wear the muffla you do it. Keep warm. Everything memory of over far I keep warm here in my heart.

I knew the pirates never left! You can see them.

Do you not know the road that go around that Pelican Cove to over town and back! Tis dusty when dry, a mud pool when wet. Usually it tis wet this time of year. I sit on the water now sometime and watch all the truck come onceinawhile get stuck in the mud! Ho! Better take to the watermuch cooler on the water.

Jeep goin on up the cliff. Steep so, you know that jeep gone fall down. But them bf catl over hills don fall down. Him Kostra don fall down his jeep. See cliffs rain cloud ride over cliffs layin out in the dory, lazin. A way for an old Jackabo to slow dying. One way or another we all get thee ladder to climb. Best to choose—

Here the first page ended. Junius set it aside, only slightly surprised by Grandfather's mention of pirates. The mention of death, in so many words, frightened him. He read on, keeping in mind the last words from the previous page: "best to choose—"

—yourself your first step. Slow and sun, slow and clouds, rain, on the water. Sleep, slow. One time, rain won waken me. Too much p punch and life. I am ready all the time. I am strong now but i take it out of me just to get the strength. Ever day I tell myself now pick up your muscles, ge tin the boatan go. Don feel bad for me. Damius, you I she and the boy have a good life together. Nothing atall tragic in death. Maybe tho in bein born.
Pirates don stay no pirates cove!
I don like the pirates.

What's he talking about? Junius wondered. Oh, Grandfahtha, please don't grow old in your mind!

Do you know them Shallows! Not just the channel wheremy boat go trew it by Serpents Pt. Not just there the Shalls. They the mouth of BigBay. Is too a mouth! Is land and Atlantic on one side of mouth and Is land and Carib Sea on other side of mouth. Mouth big grin! That i tis the mouth of the deep bay.
Right in the mouth is a wide Shallows, mebbe a mile wide. This why no big tourist ships ever able come to the Snake. With Greta and Phil parade around in Bermudas snappin pictures at you. The Snake have a necklace of coral complete aroun dits shores. Haven't I ever

tell you this before! I never know what I tell. No copy what I said to you before!

Grandfather had spoken of the deep bay and Pelican Cove and Pirates' Cove many times. But he had not written of the Shallows.

Called Shallows because it tis not very deep, of course, Junius thought.

There be one elderly tree twisted with life! Right smack in the middle of Shalls. It hold all the coral and rock there in one place, I think. A gret bed of coral and rock. You know what that do? Ha! That give foodan shelter tall kinds of fishes. To trunkfish and yellowtail, and foureye and grunt and parrot fishes. Barracuda. Feel him always just beyond where you can see through the deep. Watchin you, that devil barracuda. He don want to dahnce!

To conc and urchin, the rocks do give shelter. But whachout for urchin. It got black spines that standup stret and touch them, poison the body, oh yes. So wear tennishoes where swimming near urchin beds. Find them in the white sand bottom of Shalls clear water. Find them deep in the rocky places.

Whachout! But very delicate eating them urchin. Oh, many, many conc. Know? A mollusk inside conc. Conc the pretty big shell pink inside. Makin conc salad outuv mollusk inside. And conc stew. And fried conc, oh so good! Conc is tuff, you got to cook it some. But worth the time you take.

Like a wide tongue, so cool is the Shalls. One day I look over side of the dory and here come father turtle just in such a hurry! Gret big father turtle, name of

giant Nulio, I bet, too! I dremp of Nulio. But first, I
see gret fahtha giant turtle just in a terrible hurry! Right
under the surface, trew water so clear, you think you
can drink it, Junius son. You think fahtha turtle is come
to greet you. He go come stret for dory. Then he parade
aroun the bow. And he go on his way just aswayin
from side to side. His reggae dahnce!
    I come on the pirate.

Junius was startled to realize he was well into the
third page of Grandfather's letter. It was such a wonderful letter, and Junius could almost see those Shallows and the rocks in his mind. But then, there was
the mention again of a pirate. Junius shook his head
anxiously and frowned. He read on, clutching the pages
in both hands.

    I tied up on Magpie Bay. Like a half-moon, Magpie
Bay. Just rocks, no beach. But pretty, with lotsa wild
Palm leaning to the water. No swimmin there this time
a year, the nurse sharks come to mate or to have their
young, mebby they do both. You know the sharks are
far to port as you come in. Dont worry! I never go
near that port side, that far shore. Too rocky. Them
sharks like the big boulders there.
    Just about to have me a rest under the Manchineel.
Junius son, don't you dare eat that poison apple, no
apple! You got to cross over a short piece to get to
beach of Medusa Pt. Inlet. You cross over through a
path with old mesquite on both sides. Mesquite meet
each other above your head. Very pretty arching it
make, too, but hold heat, so hot! Mesquite have tiny
round hard yellow flowers, like tiny mouths. Oh won-

derful! Whachout for cow flops everywhere. Don wanto
stepinit. Watch out for longhorned cows, weigh a ton!
And go under a large tree. And down a soft slope. And
there you see gret Carib Sea, oh.

Oh! under gret sky and the black rock of Medusa.
And Medusa point on down the rocks to rise up to be
Medusa cliff, the head of the island.

See I'm almost trew the mesquite. Everthin so quiet.
Heat thick with red gnats. Gone rain. I can smell the
Caribbee. Hear it. I hope to die smellin the foam break-
ers way out, hitting the reef and breaking. From Medusa, you can see the outline of the big island and a
long thin island. All through the misty horizon. I think
I see the lost Antilles sometimes. Still as death. Death
behind me.

Not death. Be the pirate say, "Gettoutahere! Old
man! Fore I take my machete and chop yer ear off."
He push me from behind. Feel my heart stop. So hard
boomp! I find I'm on my knees goin, Huh! Huh! I feel
for my ears, may he not get them. My knees scratched
up on the rocks. Poor knee bones! Some cow flop on
my hands. Wipe on my shirt. Awful. It fresh stuff,
too.

I don see the pirates' faces. They lift me up under
the arms. I don look to see how they do it. But my
feet off the ground. They take me back and sling me
in the water to where I tie up my boat. I slowly get
me in the boat. Take a long time. I'm tired. Then I
hear splashin. Pirates got me again! Lift me in boat. I
don't look. Wait until they on the shore. "Never come
back, old man," they say. "Or we run you trew." So
I get out of there. Take me time to get that motor
started. I pull the cord but nothing happen for awhile

as I drift to sharkland. Anchor stop holding. But I get motor started finally.

Junius realized he was holding his breath in as he read about the pirates. He couldn't believe what he had read. And yet, as he read it over and over, he could imagine the whole scene in vivid detail. Grandfather falling hard to his knees. Surprised by thugs from behind. A sweet, old man being treated cruelly, hurt for no reason. The pirates were like vile ghosts.

"It can't be real. It can't be true!" Junius said. His worst fears seemed to have come out from some dark, hidden place into the light of truth. "Oh, be careful. Are you seein' things? Oh, he's seein' things. I hope he's seein' things. No, I don't. But wouldn't that be better than if it were real?" Junius whispered to himself. "Is he drinkin' the Punch he told us about, too much of it? Oh, Grandfahtha!"

Junius didn't know what to do. He got up from the chair, thinking to call his mother. He sat abruptly down again. And got up a second time. Then down once more. He had to finish the letter. He was on the last page.

Don worry! I know old heathen Burtie has his gun. Where he keep it. And I take it hide it in the dory. And every time I take the dory out now, I'm gon have that automatic with me and no pirate gon say where I can go and where I cannot go. I go as I please. We, pirates and me, both have our ancestors in the Caribbee. Don tell Burtie. Don wan to scare the mahn. He got his heathen ways, white sona fagun. Ha! But we keep the gun placement from him an he don need know the pirates walkin the land. Hope I don ever come pon them on Burtie Rawlings place. End of page. Sun goin down i hope not forever. urs. [signed in careful penmanship] Gran father.

Junius sat there, staring at the page. He read the whole letter through again. When at last he stirred himself, he heard a soft knock on the front door.

Oh, mahn! He put the letter on his desk and went to the door. To let his friend in. Sarrietta. Seeing her, the real world he lived in seemed more solid than ever. How could it be anything else but real with her in it?

"Hi!" she said. "You look peculiar, Junius. Is something the matter?"

And that moment he knew he would take Sarrietta into his confidence. "It's my Grandfahtha Jackabo. Got a letter from him and I am disturbed by it."

"Let's see it," she said simply.

" 'Swhat I like about you, young woman," he said, making light. His heart was heavy, though. "You come right to what makes sense, no playin' around."

She turned and gave him a beautiful grin.

"Can I kiss you, Sarrietta?" he asked softly.

"No!" she whispered. She looked surprised. "Junius, if you start to pull something like that—"

"It was just a thought," he said. He looked down at his feet, his hands deep in his pockets.

"Anyway," she said, "you don't ask a young woman that."

"You don't?" he said.

She giggled, holding her notebook against her cheek, playful again. She shook her head. "You just do it—but don't you dare!"

"I mean, I wouldn't know what to do if you had said yes, I can kiss *you*," Junius said. "I never kiss no young woman, no young lady, before." He did not lift his eyes. Something about his expression was so forlorn, Sarrietta reached out and touched his cheek.

She smiled and laughed nervously. She frowned and was silent.

"Come," he said, "say hello to Muhtha." Just then his mother came out of her bedroom and smiled down the hall at them. Sarrietta went to greet her.

Junius made himself stand straight and look pleasant, so his mother wouldn't worry about the letter now. Later, when his father came home, was soon enough.

He and Sarrietta did some studying for about a half hour. Not so very much. They didn't have a lot of homework. Mostly, they read the letter. That is, Sarrietta read it and Junius sat on the floor beside her. He felt that his parents wouldn't mind that he let her read it. She leaned closer to him. Their faces nearly touched, but he made no move toward her. He wouldn't do that.

"What do you think?" he asked.

She first had to get used to Grandfather Jackabo's handwriting and shorthand. Once that was clear, she could concentrate on what he had written. All this she told Junius.

At last she said, "Well, it's such a nice letter. It must be wonderful down there, warm all the time, the sea. But I think there might really be something wrong. Or else he has a very *large* imagination."

"That's what I thought," Junius said. He sighed. "My fahtha best see this as soon as he get home."

"I have to ask you something," Sarrietta said.

"What's that? Anything for you," he said. He didn't turn his head toward her for fear he would try to kiss her.

"Could you come to my house tomorrow and study, stay for dinner?" He was so surprised and pleased, but she didn't give him a chance to answer. "Because my mother thinks there's something funny going on between us." Sarrietta looked pained, ashamed. "I don't want her calling your mother and checking up on me."

"Oh, sure. Sure I come on over to your house, shoot, yes!" Junius said.

He made Sarrietta laugh. "Thanks," she said.

They looked into one another's eyes. Sarrietta looked down. "My house is not like yours," she said. "I'm an only child too, but it's different from here."

"How so, different?" Junius asked.

"My parents are much older," she began, and then seemed to change direction. "Everybody respects you here," she said. "Your mother and father pay attention to what you say. Even to what I say. But at home . . ." She let her voice trail off, shaking her head.

This time he did touch her, on the arm. It was a gentle, reassuring pat. "I come on oveh your house tomorrow," he told her. "Your muhtha going to love Junius Rawlings, dontcha see."

Sarrietta giggled happily. "She's going to love your accent like I do," she said.

"Sure!" he said, confidently. "And she going to want Junius son to be there, keepin' company with sweet Sarrietta every day. It tis true! You wait and see."

He couldn't believe it was happening. Sarrietta. Going over to her house.

Him. Junie-mahn. Hey-mahn! And beautiful Sarrietta Dobbs!

# Eight

Burtie went about the chore of making supper.

*"I should like to rise and go,"*

he sang, his voice a fuzzy tenor,

*"Where the golden apples grow—*

Do ye know what that is, cousin?" he asked Grandfather Jackabo.

Grandfather raised one eyebrow, only slightly surprised old heathen Burtie had called him cousin. Dirty Burtie had done that before when heady with the Planter's Punch, in the best of their times together.

*"I should like to rise and go,"*

Burtie began again, awfully out of tune,

*"Where the golden apples grow;*
*Where below another sky*

*Parrot islands anchored lie*
*And, watched by cockatoos and goats,*
*Lonely Crusoes building boats . . .*

"Do ye know it, son!" Burtie asked, his look tender with emotion.

"Cannot say I do," Jackabo said. The mahn's in a peaceable mood, he thought. Well he should be. Tis a rapturous evenin' as I've ever seen, thought Grandfather Jackabo.

The sun posed atop the western hills, blazing rude and raucous for all to see. It washed the greens and browns away and drenched every height in gold. The sky was a vibrant, perfect blue.

"That's an old Robby Louie Stevenson poem, dontcha know," dirty Burtie said. "I put it to music, mysel. And ever hear tell of Parrot Islands, you?" he asked Stinking Black Jack.

Grandfather Jackabo thought about it. Parrot Islands! "I daresay where the birds live in abundance," he said at last. Feeling both happy and worn out; the Planter's Punch did that.

"Aye, Stinking Jack, ye guessed it right. Gret lot o' birds o' Tobago and Trinidad. We were there once, do ye remember it? Naw, surely not. Yer too old and that was long ago, dontcha know!"

Grandfather Jackabo remembered something. He went quite still inside. And as if sitting on a bench somewhere, he watched a memory slide by: revelers, dancing and singing calypso favorites. Heat, scorching the mind. Men wearing giant yellow, pink, and black butterflies on their heads. One man had transformed himself into a huge pink-and-gold peacock. Other men were masked African warriors. Women in turquoise, silver, gold sequins, like magical mermaids come to glide over the land. It was the week before Lent, and Carnival had burst into costume on the streets of Trinidad.

Jackabo watched the memory fade. He said nothing about it to heathen Burtie. Why bother? He was content to be where he was. Sometimes he could sit there, his bare feet resting in the indentations on the cool cement floor where many a slave lad had placed his feet. Waited, the lads had, for the steaming supper dishes to carry up to the big house. Jackabo would feel himself drawing in. He became even smaller than a lad. He became no bigger than a sparrow hawk, the kind that had nested among the stone huts of the hundreds of slaves who toiled to make the rum, sugar, and molasses that brought riches to the white Rawlingses. Tales of the sparrow hawks had been handed down, another part of Jackabo's slave ancestry.

And now Grandfather Jackabo spread his wings.

Stinking Black Jack, with his arms held wide apart and flapping, was what heathen Burtie saw as he glanced around from his work at the stove. He understood the old time of Black Jack's mind. "So now yer a bird o' prey, are ye, cousin?" he said. "Well, be a hawk then, let's see ye fly! Oh, ye don't wanter! Time to roost, is it? Then sit still there, birdy, this junk don't taste too bad after all."

Grandfather Jackabo sat contentedly at his end of the long, black table framed in bamboo. He sniffed the food and his mouth watered. His chair was made of bamboo as well, its cushion so old that the cotton tick was as smooth as silk.

The kitchen was a separate building. It was made of stone to the height of three feet. The rest of it was a red pitched roof supported by beams, and open walls on three sides. The fourth side was walled up against the hillside. In the slave days, food passed through the wall openings from stone ovens.

Now Burtie had finally screened in the walls. Grandfather could sit at the table in front of the largest open wall and not one mosquito could find him. Still, the tiny mimis got in through the screening every time food was cooked. They got in your ears and up your nose. They surrounded the heat. Got singed and fell into boiling and frying food. Best to cover everything until the last minutes of browning. They were so tiny, those mimis, that Jackabo or Burtie hardly noticed them. They might as well have been pepper, they were that small.

All the Rawlings Estate buildings and ruins that remained of the once-proud plantation were on various levels of the hillside. Only the kitchen was directly below and to the right of the big house. It was the one building where the roof didn't leak. Everything leaked in the big house. Burtie had managed to caulk and seal their bedrooms off the forecourt. It was all right for the rain to come in their screen doors. It was the leaks over the beds that they minded. Still, one had to take care about the scorpions. And it was many a morning that Grandfather Jackabo, forgetting where he was, would pull out of bed barefoot, only to step on a heathen giant black waterbug.

"Call them what you will, mahn," he told heathen Burtie. "Them things is extraord'nary big misters cockroaches."

"They are waterbugs, is all," Burtie told him back. "Harmless."

"They are monstrous flying cock*roaches* come right in my face, and I hate them and I wishin' they would drown in the Caribbee!" trembling, Grandfather had said.

"Let's eat, Black Jack," Burtie said now.

"Ah!" cried Grandfather Jackabo. He clapped his hands once together. That meant all was well with him. He needn't move. Burtie had taken care of everything.

They had come from the dock in one bad sweat, too. They had showered under the hose spray that came directly from the cistern spigot. The west wall of the deep cement cistern was exposed to the heat of the afternoon sun. The cistern was full of rainwater.

Soft water. And that water came out of the spigot quite warm for about thirty seconds. Long enough! They had good showers together, not even poking fun or, worse, being angry. Getting the salt-sea smell and the perspiration off was what they were about.

Heathen, dirty Burtie had changed his shirt, at least, and now wore a faded brown *guayabera*, that straight-cut shirt of the tropics. He looked almost dignified, with his hair all slicked down, was Grandfather's opinion.

Grandfather Jackabo had on an old blue work shirt once belonging to Junius son, until his monk's-cloth shirting dried fresh. He'd washed it out with the hose and hung it on the line in back of the tool shed. One needed no more than two or three shirts for the tropic heat. It wouldn't do ever to wear something new.

Tis odd, he thought, wearin' clothes the same as a boy would wear. Am I not a child again!

"I'm not old," he said out loud to heathen Burtie. "I'm a lad again."

"That's yer problem, all right," Burtie answered. "But ye ain't got the sense of even a lad, ye old devil!"

"Huh!" Grandfather said. "You know nothing."

"Huh, yersel! I know this *arroz* is good and hot, too."

Burtie brought the pot of yellow rice right from the stove and placed it on the table. He placed a bowl of hot black beans next to it. Then he brought a tureen full of his hamburger and tomato mixture.

"Ah, smells like heaven," Grandfather sighed, sniffing the steam from the dishes.

"So ye've been to heaven, too," said heathen Burtie.

"I'll be there before you ever will," Grandfather said.

"Right ye are, with one of yer big feet in the grave already," said Burtie, chuckling to himself.

He brought two stumps of white candles to the table and lit them before he sat down.

Grandfather Jackabo clapped his hands as the yellow light flickered and held. They would have light once the sun was gone behind the hills. There was no electric light in the kitchen. They cooked on the gas stove, using bottled gas. The sun was going now, for sure, Grandfather noticed. But not for good.

"Be back tomorrow!" he said, grinning at the hills.

Burtie scraped his chair and sat, turning to see what Stinking Jack was grinning at. "Aye, the sun," he said at last. "Now wouldn't it be somethin' if it didn't come up tomorrow, nor never after tomorrow, too?"

"Would be nothin'," said Grandfather, "for it always do come up again."

"Not tomorrow, it don't. I know for a fact, it ain't comin' up tomorrow."

All at once, Grandfather's back stiffened, for a chill ran up his spine, as though the ancient Devil were near and about to take the hindmost. Which would mean he would take the last, the slowest, and that would mean Grandfather, himself.

"Don't ever say that!" he whispered to heathen Burtie. "Never curse such as the sun!"

"I know for a fact," dirty Burtie went on teasing. "Tomorrow will be dark as hell. And cold as ice. That Pelican Cove down there will be good only for iceskatin'. The hills will break open because it's forty below zero and ye'll breathe the freezin' sulphur stench that's inside 'em—hee hee!"

"Stop it! Please, Burtie, don't dare the Devil!" Grandfather was beside himself. A sweat broke on his brow. He clutched Burtie's arm; the food was still steaming, but cooling. He didn't know why he was so terrified all of a sudden. He simply knew he must stop Burtie.

"Aye," Burtie said at last. "Let go o' me now. I ain't said nothing. Okay now." He patted Grandfather's shoulder. It was an awkward gesture, for he was not one to soothe another, particularly a black. "Calm yersel now. Leggo my arm, mahn. What's come over ye?"

"You must not curse the sun here, on this hillside," answered Grandfather Jackabo.

"And why not—when it tis my own hillside?" asked Burtie, still playing, but afraid now of upsetting Stinking Black Jack again. No telling when an old mahn would die. He didn't want to be the direct cause of that.

"Because." Grandfather thought a moment. "Twas my kind clear from Africa that toiled beneath that there sun. They laid their curses down here on this very ground. For one, two centuries, they did. They cursed the day all white Rawlingses be born. The sun may have heard them and kept the curse for them. For they be African children of the sun."

"Huh," said Burtie. "Such imagination, such fears! So I am damned, am I? Well, so be it." He turned back to the sun. Its last flame lit the trees at the hilltop behind the house of Gerard Kostera.

Suddenly Burtie stood in a crouch and shook his fist at the sun, hooting, "Lie down, ye red dog! Lie down and stay down! Out of my sight, ye hear? Aye, bring me the moon. I like the moon better!"

Grandfather Jackabo could feel the moon rising behind the ruined Rawlings manor house. The moon was an eye, surely, coolly watching.

He shook his head. "You do us no good," he said to heathen Burtie. "There's only so much hell a hill can hold down."

"Oh, shatap and eat!" Burtie said. He spooned the rice onto Stinking Jack's plate. He sprinkled black beans on top of that. Then he poured the hamburger sauce over it all. "There," he said. "Curse yer tongue with that."

Soon they were eating away. The only sounds between them were the sounds of their enjoyment.

"Tis good!" whispered Grandfather between swallowing. "You need to do more food makin' like this."

"I hate cooking," said heathen Burtie. "A man o' my kind never had to cook."

The rest of the meal was silence, broken by Burtie rising now and again to fill their glasses with Planter's Punch. Grandfather knew he should not drink too much before going to bed. Soon after nightfall, they would take to their beds and rise with the morning birdcalls.

Grandfather discovered that his plate was clean. He did not remember eating everything. "I want more," he told heathen Burtie.

"You had two helpings already," Burtie told him.

Grandfather thought about that. He did feel full. He just didn't remember. "Then I'll have me some ice cream." His pleasure was for Junius to fix him chocolate ice cream.

"Ye know we don't have no ice cream," heathen Burtie said. "By the time we get it back here from town, it'd be all melted. The best I can do for ye is some Jell-O."

Burtie got the Jell-O. He brought it down from the big house. It was lime and lemon mixed, and it was melting. He placed the bowl of it and a spoon before Grandfather.

Grandfather ate it and forgot he had. When he looked, his bowl was empty.

"Well, give me some!" he told heathen Burtie.

"Ye done et it all, ye black, stinkin' mahn! Ye get no more or ye'll be sick. Now go to bed. Wait. I'll lead ye up when I'm finished here. Can't trust ye atall no more."

Obediently, Grandfather Jackabo waited. He knew he should help with the clearing away of the dishes and washing and drying them. But he found he had no will to move. He was mostly paralyzed, holding on to his glass. It was empty again. Danged if he could keep his plates and things full this night. The Devil was due, he was sure of it. He tried to prepare himself, but he could not help shivering.

Dirty Burtie hurried, cleaning up. Out of the corner of his eye, he watched the old black fool. What's he shakin' about in all this heat? Is the mahn fell off his rocker? Well, I've about made up my mind. He's got to go back. I can't be responsible for him climbin' and fallin' off a hill or drownin' from the boat. What do they expect of me, and me a white mahn, too? It's not like he was young as me and getting around good. What am I, a nursemaid? I say they got it all turned round!

Grandfather Jackabo felt the passage of time like a soft breeze across his face. He felt himself moving, climbing, and there was a white light over everything, but he had no memory of why he was moving. The next that he saw, he was lying in his bed. Lying stiff as a board, and for a moment he thought he was a dead man. He looked at one stiff arm and then the other. When he realized he was moving his head, he knew he was still alive.

Burtie, I'm sick. He did not say this out loud. He thought he had, but he hadn't.

Come, Burtie, I need to walk awhile. Will you walk with me? Burtie? Burtie? Answer me, mahn.

Grandfather cried out inside. What if you're the one is sick, mahn. Do you feel all right, dirty Burtie? Do you? Oh, mahn. Don't give me no more Punch. Each time, I think it's going to be fine. It just like fruit juice, the way it go down. I feel strong when I drink it. And then, suddenly, somethin' happen to me. Gawd! I'll lie here and wait 'til mornin'. Then you'll come and it will be all right, dontcha see.

Grandfather was suspended, with the breeze of time caressing his cheek. He felt a shivering up and down his body, and he pulled the sheet up to his chin. He slept fitfully. Sometime in the moonlit night he awoke, as awake as he could get with the Punch power boiling his blood.

Huh? What? Someone had spoken. A man cried out. He did not actually hear a cry. Maybe it had passed him on the breeze that time made as it traveled onward. He listened. He got out of bed and walked toward the door. Both his and Burtie's sleeping rooms were former house slave quarters that had been added on long ago. They opened onto the ruined forecourt of the old mansion. There was a screen door to each room. When rains came, they came right in. But that was fine. The tiled floors were then cleansed, and they dried quickly from the heat of the day.

Someone was coming. Grandfather was about to call dirty Burtie's name when there occurred the Devil's business, right before his eyes.

In the moonlight, walking along the court outside, were men. At first he thought they might be former slaves. But then, oh, Grandfather knew them. Oh, yes! One had poor heathen Burtie slung down his back. Carried dirty Burtie like he was a sack o' meal, he did. They were one and the same pirates that had bothered Grandfather just a while ago. He thought he had written Junius son about them. But he hadn't known then they were in the Devil's power. Come to carry out the curse of the old ones who were black, and slaves. There was nothing Grandfather could do to stop the pirates, even if he could have moved.

He kept forgetting where he was. First he thought he was still in bed, watching a memory pass before his eyes. Next he thought it was day, morning, and he was going in to call Burtie. Then, somehow, he was standing, seeing the moonlight, and he knew by its cold brightness on the dark waters of Pelican Cove that the time must be well past midnight.

Grandfather Jackabo found himself in bed. He fell asleep again almost at once. When he awoke, it was truly morning. Birds, chattering annoyingly close. His mind was clean of the Devil's work. Memory of the night had gone with the dark.

# Nine

Junius and Sarrietta were downtown, gazing up at the Noel tree in the fading light of late afternoon. Their hats and coats were covered with snowflakes. The snow was above their ankles. Nobody had bothered to shovel the sidewalks yet. Junius didn't mind.

*"Tis the season to be jolly,*
*Fa-la-la-la-la la-la-la-la"*

played from a loudspeaker on the side of the bank. It was twelve days before Christmas. All the downtown business storefronts were decorated with Christmas trees, Christmas lights, and ornaments. There was a gigantic fir tree that grew in the triangular green space in front of the town offices. Each year it became the town's Noel tree. Just yesterday Christmas balls as large as snowballs were hung from the tree. Workmen added blue and yellow and red lights in long, vertical strands that went on and off in series. What made the tree even more Christmasy was that it was covered with real, fresh snow that reflected the colors of the lights. The snow had been falling since early morning, and it was still falling. Snowplows were out, making their serious, heavy noise and throwing snow in piles at curbside.

Junius enjoyed seeing the tree lights, while the sound of automobiles thud-thudded, passing over the packed snow out on the street. There was nothing quite like the first few days of the Christmas season. Fresh decorations and fresh snow!

"I wish we could stay out here until it gets good and dark. Then the tree will really look nice," said Sarrietta.

"It's looking okay right now," Junius said. "You would surely freeze by dark, too. Girls freeze ever so much faster than boys, dontcha see?" he told her.

Sarrietta laughed. "But boys melt faster in the summertime," she said, giggling.

He smiled at that. "Don't know about no summertime meltin', see," he said. "It be wintertime now, Christmastime now, when all girls freeze. Got to watch one of them ever so close. And she makin' Junius son melt every minute. He cannot help himself." He looked down into her sweet face. Everything be so sweet these days, he thought. I just love everything, so good and sweet!

Junius knew he had to get Sarrietta home. It was getting late. They had been fooling around downtown since school was out at two fifteen. It was Early Tuesday, too, when school let out an hour earlier to allow teachers to catch up on paperwork. Early Tuesday came the second and fourth Tuesdays of every month. Junius appreciated Early Tuesday more than ever now, for it gave him a longer time with Sarrietta.

They had sat by themselves for a while in one of the booths in Mary and Slim's. Then the booth had filled with Sarrietta's friends. He would not call them his friends yet. They still treated him as though he were an alien being whom Sarrietta had become infatuated with but would soon get over. Maybe it was true. But right now he didn't care if it was.

The kids crowded into the booth to watch and wait. He didn't mind that, either. Because even though the booth was full, he and Sarrietta remained alone. They were interested in one another. He hadn't asked her to be his girl, not yet. It was obvious to him that she was. They had been seeing one another now for almost two weeks. He had kissed her more than once. The first time furtively by their lockers at school. They had both been late getting to school, and had run into one another at the lockers. The last bell had already sounded and the hall had been empty. He had simply taken her by the arm, leaned down as she looked up inquiringly at him, and kissed her.

Looking in those eyes, he thought now. Lips, so soft. Girl, I like you so. Don't get mad with me.

She hadn't been angry. She had taken a tiny step

backward and had broken the kiss. Once in a while he kissed her. And she let him. He was careful that no one saw. And yet some few must have seen, the way the students watched them now. But all that mattered to Junius was that Sarrietta liked him. He would imagine, in a flight of fancy, that she loved him.

In the booth, the two of them were crammed against one another. There were four kids to a side and three or four more had dragged chairs over to sit. There was noise, shouting, teasing, woofing, and laughter. He and Sarrietta were mostly quiet. She smiled around, but didn't say much. He said nothing at all. Junius paid no attention to the others. He was learning how to act cool. They were just kids, students, not worth thinking about, his superior attitude toward them seemed to say. Where once he had wished so hard to be accepted by them, he cared nothing about that now. How his days had changed!

He had Sarrietta's hand clasped tightly in his under the table. She had her head leaning against his shoulder. He didn't mind being her leaning post. He could look down at her, over her. He was her protector.

Wonder what would happen if I kissed her now in front of everybody, he thought. That wouldn't do atall. It would be makin' a public spectacle. She not like any public display of affection, you know. She is very proper and that's good. Never do anything to make her unhappy.

Sarrietta raised her head and whispered in his ear.

He looked at her, whispered back. The loud talk at the table broke off as the kids strained to hear. Junius knew what they must be thinking, that he and Sarrietta were romancing. He knew how they would let their imaginations run wild.

Sarrietta whispered again. Junius looked at her, deep in her eyes, and nodded. He could feel the kids taking it all in. He forced himself not to laugh, but to pretend.

All she had said was that she had better get home. "Junius, we better go," she had whispered. "We need to look over some G-O and maybe the Lorca poem in Spanish."

He'd whispered back. "Anytime you are ready, Sarrietta, I take you home."

"I'm ready now—let's get out of here!" she had said. He had nodded and they left.

"Come on, girl," Junius told Sarrietta now. "You standing here snow blind and Noel blind and time be wastin'. You know what time it tis, girl?"

"Time? Me-e! You're the one's wasting *my* time!" Sarrietta said. But she was joking. Just exaggerating an angry posture.

"It tis nearly four o'clock," he said.

"Uh-oh, hope Mother doesn't remember this is Early Tuesday," she said.

"Don't worry, I'll take care of Muhtha," Junius said smugly.

She laughed. "Junius, you are scared of my mother."

He looked pained, shocked. "I, Junius son, am scared

of no*bahdy*. I, Junius son, have Muhtha lovin' Junius so much, she think she got to sit there and look at him the whole time he study with Sarrietta."

Sarrietta was smiling happily, her arm linked with his as they hurried away from the Christmas-downtown toward home. "She sit there watchin' Junius 'cause she don't trust Junius with her daughter," Sarrietta said, mocking his speech. "You're just mad she won't let us study in my room." She grinned at him, jumping, bouncing through the snow at his side.

He made a snowball and threw it at her. It came apart, the snow was that dry and fluffy. Sarrietta screamed anyway.

"Huh. Your muhtha a sick woman," he said, half joking.

"She's smart enough to know-oh not to let you in my ro-om," Sarrietta sang.

"Hush, girl, 'fore I smack you in the mouth—like this." He went quickly to kiss her but she was quicker.

She dodged in front of him. "I won't walk with you, fresh!" she said.

He pouted and she was soon at his side again.

The time alone with her went all too quickly for Junius. It seemed only a moment and they were at the corner of her block. He had carried her books and his own in a new gym duffel bag he had bought just for that purpose, all the way from school to downtown, and all the way back. And he hadn't realized he had the bag at all. It hadn't felt heavy or anything. He had gloves on. His hands were cold, but he didn't mind that either. His shoes were wet, his feet numb at the toes, but who cared? Sarrietta wore pretty boots. Smart Sarrietta, he thought.

At the walk up to the front steps and porch, Junius stopped. "Girl," he said, "why don't we duck behind this snowy bush here a moment—"

"Junius! Shhhh!" Sarrietta whispered.

"Have a little kiss or two—"

"Junius! Stop playing. You're going to get me in trouble."

"Your muhtha think you a two-year-old. And she think boys are four-year-old monsters, too."

"Junius, she's my mother. Please."

Junius sighed. "Okay, you are right about that," he said. "And any muhtha of Sarrietta is all right with me. No kidding. No playin' around, mahn. I love Missus Dobbs, so. I think she the best lady I ever met. She a fine smart woman, dontcha—"

Sarrietta broke in: "I don't think you should joke about my mother like that."

"All right, you're right. I'm sorry. I'll be a good four-year-old, just the way she wants," he said. He could tell Sarrietta didn't like that, but she didn't say anything. She led the way inside. He steeled himself against the cold and correct Mrs. Marcella Dobbs. His own father might be very formal acting, but he was not cold. No, not ever, Junius thought.

Junius didn't even pause in the living room to look

at the newly decorated Christmas tree. He went directly to the dining room. Mrs. Dobbs was there before he got there. She had heard them come in.

"Well," she called, "you're late." Spoken around Junius to Sarrietta hanging her coat in the hall closet.

Not a "Good afternoon," or a "Hello, how are you, daughter?" Junius thought. Not a "Good day" to Junius son. Never offering me a drink of water or milk. Never sayin' "Hello" or "Good-bye." Just watching, sometimes, sittin' there beside the doorway, just inside the room. While her precious daughter get free lessons from Junius son. She think I'm a fool. I don't know she think I'm only good for tutoring? And the mahn part she got to keep an eye on? Well, you right, Missus. Better keep a sharp eye out, for Junius going to steal your lovely daughter. Going call her his own, any minute now.

Junius stood there by the table, his gym bag in his hand, with his coat on. He squeezed the handle of the bag so hard, his fingers ached. Here was a tactic, just planned. He would force Mrs. Dobbs to at least give a nod to him. He kept his eyes fastened to hers. A faint smile on his lips.

Sarrietta came into the dining room. "Junius, let me hang up your coat. It's dripping wet."

He made no move to put his bag down and take off his coat. "I don't know if I can stay very long. Maybe fifteen minutes. I just leave the coat on," he said.

"But we have to study!" Sarrietta said, alarmed.

He slowly took his eyes from her mother, standing there, watching and listening, to look at Sarrietta. *You have to study*, he made his look speak. Suddenly he felt very hard inside, very cold toward this mother and daughter. He didn't know where the feeling had come from.

He turned back to Mrs. Dobbs, intercepting an angry look from Sarrietta to her mother as he did so. He would not quite meet the mother's gaze.

"I'll take your coat," Mrs. Dobbs said abruptly.

Yes, that's it, he thought. You will take my coat, Missus Mean. He put down the bag. Taking his time, he carefully took off his gloves and coat.

You never seen Junius son be a nasty four-year-old? he thought. Well, he can certainly be.

"I'll make some hot chocolate," Mrs. Dobbs said, turning to her daughter.

"Thank you, Mother," Sarrietta said.

"Oh, none for me," Junius said, touching Mrs. Dobbs' arm. Her skin felt crisp, like dry paper. She seemed more like a grandmother than a mother, he thought. She swung around with his coat, as if he had hurt her.

"Sarrietta and I had malts downtown at Mary and Slim's." He spoke easily. "Early Tuesday, dontcha know," he said, smiling. Caught the warning look from Sarrietta but he didn't care. "Have you seen the decorations downtown?"

He waited, forcing Mrs. Dobbs to answer, as she digested the information that this was Early Tuesday, that they had been together for the last two hours.

"No . . . no, I haven't been down there," said Mrs. Dobbs. "Sarrietta knows she is to come home right after school. We don't allow her to fool around downtown."

"Mother, I'm not a baby," Sarrietta said softly.

"Well, Sarrietta wasn't down there by herself," Junius said, politely. "I was there to protect her." He smiled graciously at Mrs. Dobbs and continued. "You really should see the Noel tree, mahm, it tis such a beautiful sight. Sarrietta love it so. We stand there for ten minutes at least while she drink it in. Ha-ha." And then with simple ease, he reached out and touched Sarrietta's cheek, as though to brush away some invisible mark. It was an affectionate gesture as well. Next, he just as easily took her hand in his. Squeezed it as she and her mother stared at him.

So what will you do now, Missus? Embarrass your beautiful daughter? Risk having the tutor leave? In the back of his mind, he realized he was being rather harsh. But he didn't like being insulted, and Sarrietta's mother was often insulting.

In the silence he let go of Sarrietta's hand and emptied the duffel full of their books on the dining room table. "Sarrietta, let us get started," he said.

He didn't know when Mrs. Dobbs went out of the room. He didn't care. He was sitting and Sarrietta was sitting close, next to him and the rectangular table. He looked up at her and grinned.

"You sure are something!" she whispered beside him.

"So? What I'm supposed to do, let her treat me like nothin'?"

"She doesn't treat you like nothing," Sarrietta whispered.

"Stop whisperin', for goodness' sakes," he said, in an even voice.

"You'll make her angry!" she said.

I don't care, he thought. "Look, let's get started. I do have work of my own to do."

She was pouting; she grabbed the G-O book and flung it open. "I hate this stuff. If I didn't need it for college I would drop it!"

"Not everybody need to go to college," he said.

"I have as much right to go to college as you!"

"You have some right," he said, holding back a grin, "but I have much more right, and need, being a mahn."

He ducked and laughed. She had nearly flung the book at him. "You chauvinist!" she cried. "I hate you."

"Girls better to cook and sew and make the gar-*den* grow!"

"Oooh, you chauvinist pig!" And she hit him with the book.

"Darn me, she going to beat me up, she so tough. Hee-hee!" He was shielding his head, pretending to be scared.

"Oooh, I hate you!"

In a second, he had taken the book from her. "You are weak, girl. How you going to fight any*bahdy*?" And then he had her by both hands. She struggled but she couldn't get loose. "There," he said softly. "Now. Behave. Or I kiss you again!"

"Junius! Don't!"

"Right before Muhtha's eyes!" He pecked her on the cheek.

Mrs. Dobbs was coming. "Sarrietta, I have your hot chocolate," she called.

Woman always announced her arrival. Like some queen, Junius thought.

When she came in, they were busy studying. Junius was talking softly to Sarrietta. He had his arm over the back of her chair but he was not touching her. He could feel Mrs. Dobbs observing how closely they sat, their heads lowered to the books. She paused before setting down two cups and a pot of chocolate.

"A quadrilateral with exactly one pair of parallel sides is called a what?" Junius asked.

"A trapezoid," Sarrietta said.

"Okay, then. The parallel sides are what?" Junius asked.

Silence. Then, "The parallel sides are bases—and the two nonparallel sides are legs," she said.

"Good," he said. Mrs. Dobbs set the cups and saucers and the pot down. Junius paused long enough to pour himself and Sarrietta chocolate. He had changed his mind about having it. He did not look up at Mrs. Dobbs.

"And if the legs of a trapezoid are congruent, the quadrilateral is called? What?"

"Isosceles?" Sarrietta said.

"An isosceles trapezoid," he said. "So consider the following experiment over here. It tis one of the problems due tomorrow," he said, pointing to the next page and a drawing of a trapezoid.

Mrs. Dobbs went out. "I won," Junius whispered in Sarrietta's ear.

Sarrietta shrugged.

"You like Jimi Hendrix?" he asked.

For a second, she looked startled by the question. But then she said, "I like Prince better."

Junius groaned. "You can still like Hendrix," he said. "Next time you come over, I will play Jimi for you."

"Didn't Jimi Hendrix die?" she asked.

He sighed and sang Hendrix to her:

> *"I made up my mind.*
> *I'm tired of wastin' my precious time.*
> *You've got to be mine,*
> *Foxy lady!"*

The way Junius sang it, the song had a reggae beat.

"Jimi Hendrix never die," Junius murmured in her ear.

# Ten

It was not a bad day for Grandfather Jackabo. It was not exactly a good one, either. It was the day that he noticed a strange quiet on the Rawlings Estate. Jackabo could not move around the lands very quickly. Morning was not his best time. He lay in bed, feeling the arthritic pain in his shoulders and down his back. He gauged its strength and the length of time it would take him to work it from his arm muscles. He needed his arms. He was amazed at just how much he needed them whenever he lost the use of them to aching joint pain.

He was listening hard to the silence; it reminded him of something he had forgotten. Jackabo Rawlings was not quite sure he was awake.

"Must've had too much of the Punch; it punchin' *me*," he told himself. His throat was dry. He had an awful taste in his mouth. And he'd forgotten to remove his false teeth.

He took them out and dropped them in the glass of solution he always kept on a small table by his bed. They seemed to grin rather sadly at him.

I will have to brush them hard, he thought. A mahn does need teeth in the daytime, dontcha see, for his self-respect. It will not do to wait for teeth to cleanse themselves. The thought made him chuckle.

Jackabo tried to lift what it was he'd forgotten from the heavy fog in his brain. "Twill come to me," he said quietly. "It does always come back to me, after time, one way or another."

Something was different. Grandfather thought about that a moment. The hour was well after six, he knew, for he felt the heat that had begun to rise from the hillside. It flowed like liquid across the forecourt to the brick walls of his bedroom. Already the one window in the front wall was bright with daylight. Oh, very bright. When Grandfather squinted, he could pretend the light was some shiny ornament on a huge Christmas tree. Home was in his mind, he found, and the winter holiday season. Not this home, but the one way over far, where lived the boy, Junius son, and his own boy, Damius, and Jaylene, daughter-in-law. Then he thought of snow and slippery ice, and felt a chill wind in his soul.

"I cannot live out my days where tis so cold," he whispered to the shape of sadness creeping near. Something he'd forgotten, hidden in the shape.

Grandfather Jackabo lay straight and still under the

sheet. Only his hands moved, as he opened and closed them, testing the tightness of his arm muscles. Soon he would lift both his arms up and out and down. That always made him wince; but it was the second step toward getting the pain out of his shoulders.

Burtie must have overslept, Jackabo thought. The mahn had not come to wake him soon after sunup. They always went to bed an hour or so after dark and rose early the next day. It was the way of the tropics and nature's own way in the islands. Dirtie Burtie there, shouting at the screen door. Grandfather Jackabo laughed. That was how the mahn looked! Heathen Burtie, standing at the screen and shouting at it.

"Dirty Burtie, hollerin' at the screen door. That's how it look," Grandfather murmured. "Just day before yes'dy, there I be, layin' on the bed, there he come, shuffling along saying so loud, 'Get ye up, ye Stinking Black! Jack! Ye think this be yer born day and ye can sleep-a-bed the whole daylight? Get tup! Get tup! The *gandules* is ripe, mahn. I need ye to pick me the gandules!' " Grandfather laughed toothlessly.

Where was dirty Burtie this morning, and the gandules, little sweet pigeon peas, truly ripe now? He walk into town, maybe, Grandfather thought, though old Burtie does not do that in many a week. I go in for us in the dory. Or he feel like going with me, though he don't like the bay no more. Once we get caught in a squall of rain so bad, you couldn't see, and that scare him so.

*See the brown boobies!* I tell him another time. *They got some young with them, growin' up, dontcha see?* But he don't like no pelicans, the boobies. Burtie don't like nothing. But maybe he does like me. No, he don't. He tolerate me. He used to havin' me here now.

Maybe dirty Burtie don't like me no more.

The worrisome thought made Grandfather Jackabo weary.

Maybe that be why he not come by this mornin'. Best to ask him one time. .

"Burtie? Burtie?" Grandfather called. "I'm gettin' up, you heathen Burtie. Don't bother come shoutin' at my screen door. Ha, ha!"

It took Grandfather some time, but at last he had loosened his arm muscles enough to support himself getting out of bed. He swung his bow legs over the side and sat, looking at the floor, aware of the pain in his upper torso. He pushed it far back in his mind. He studied the floor all around, making sure there were no flying cock*roaches* about this morning, and no scorpions or tarantulas. He rarely saw Father Tarantula.

One had to dig in the guinea grass or cut it, and then one might see a furry Father Tarantula. Father Tarantula was most shy and loved the deep places. The grass would have to be cut sometime soon. He and Burtie, working together with machetes. They would wear gloves and long shirts, and trousers tied tightly at the ankles. They would work in rhythm, like twins. They would work slowly, resting often, like old men. They would fall asleep in the shade, like brothers. And they would come upon the tarantulas later, as they cut on around the hill. The thought of their huge size made Grandfather shiver.

*Ah, tarantulas ain't even half poison, the ugly son of a guns!* Burtie had told him.

*I hear tell they can make a mahn dahnce himself crazy,* Grandfather had said.

*Old lies, old native tales, dontcha know, Black Jack. Believe nothing ye hear on this island. All stories. No truth nowhere no more,* said old Burtie.

But them yellow-orange ones is worst, Jackabo thought. Ah me! Don't let the yellow spiders scent old Jack Rawlings, can't find dirty Burtie!

"Are you still abed, Burtie?" Grandfather hollered. No answer. He sighed.

It took old Jackabo some time to complete the process of grooming himself for the day. After that he usually made his and Burtie's beds. Burtie would fix them an ample breakfast of pancakes and bacon, or French toast, or eggs and bacon, depending on what had been available in the groceries. For everything came in once a week by ferryboat, and he who was quick and had money enough could get the fresh bread and sweet, and the best produce. Before the weekend sailors got it all, too.

If Burtie's gone somewhere, I will do everything myself, thought Jackabo. Big breakfast is not so good in the heat. I will have cold cereal. Yes, that will be fine this day, if Burtie stays gone away. Maybe he just sleeping late.

For some reason Jackabo felt reluctant to go see.

He had managed by will and degrees of movement to force the arthritis down his body to his legs. He would capture it in his leg muscles, which were the strongest part of him. And then he would limp it around in the tropic heat.

I'll get Burtie up and make our beds later, he thought, when I've loosened my back a bit more. Something I've forgotten! came to him again.

Need to go to the clothesline and find my cloak, he thought. He always felt better wearing the tunic. I will certainly do that, after I putting on fresh trousers. Why clothesline, my cloak? Because I wash it—yes, I remember.

The trousers were steel gray and wrinkled, but they were clean. Grandfather kept his trousers on metal pegs dirty Burtie had hammered into the mortar between the bricks of one bedroom wall. Next, he took the glass of solution with his teeth in it to the bathroom to brush them. The bathroom was the only working one. The four in the great, ruined house were out of order, and Burtie wouldn't spare the expense of having them repaired. The bathroom was down a covered passageway on one side of which were their bedrooms. The rooms and the bathroom were connected to the rest of the house by the passageway and a narrow, steep back staircase. The staircase led to another level and another corridor to the great dining room of the big house. The forecourt quarters had been free servants' quarters long after they were house slave quarters.

Carefully, Jackabo cleaned his teeth in the sink and placed them back in his mouth. He grinned at himself in the mirror. He contemplated what to do with the trousers he had lived in the whole previous day and had slept in all night. They were crumpled on the floor at his feet.

I'll leave them there, he thought. Burtie's a great pest about washin' laundry. He cannot resist pickin' up trousers to be washed on his way around and about. Then I'll know if he's just hiding from me out of spite. Mean Burtie does not stand above a grudge, no indeed! thought Grandfather. And slipping on his boating sandals, he stepped outside onto the overgrown, abandoned forecourt.

The outdoors was white with sunlight. The hills shimmered magically as Grandfather Jackabo squinted at them, adjusting his sight to the sudden brilliance. The heat was fragrant with flowers. There was hardly a breeze, a warning that the Rawlings hillside would soon be unbearably hot. As his eyes adjusted, he saw that there were light ripples on the quiet cove and bay beyond. The deep bay looked like ocean, distant. The cove was turquoise, with mild swells. He could see for miles. There were white stars of frangipani and the purple, orange, and pink of bougainvillea all along the shore, halfway down the cliffs. The gnarled trees with round leaves, called sea grapes, were at a height above the mangroves at the water's edge. Hills, cliffs, the coast road. Kostera house. Grandfather studied the house, but it was silent, as usual. He wondered why old Burtie thought so much of that house—he watched it all the time. He don't think I know, Grandfather thought.

There was misty light across the big bay, far off. It was a beautiful tropic morning, like almost every morning. The sky was clear blue. The silence was serene. Even his eyesight was better in the clear light.

"D'ya see that, Burtie?" said Jackabo. He was not three feet away from Burtie's screen door now. "The sunshine, the day does be out and about. It waitin' for you, old heathen. Well, don't answer me. See if I care!"

Grandfather stomped on his way to the clothesline. The way led down old and worn steps to the toolshed on another level. The clothesline was strung beside the shed. "Burtie?" Grandfather whispered, peering in the open door. He felt foolish, looking for heathen Burtie in the shed. Burtie wasn't there, either. Dah. *Dah* came to Grandfather. It was the West Indian dialect for "there." Burtie no dah, he thought.

He took his cloak from the line where there were a few towels hanging. It was stiff and very warm. He put it on over his head. Ah, yes! The heat of it on his back and arms was just what he needed.

Slowly, Jackabo straightened all the way. The stiffness was certainly going. In the sunlight, the heat was soon a tonic; his legs ached only a little. Grandfather smoothed his hands down the front of his cloak and over the arms and headed back up to the forecourt. Gandules grew all around the old steps. The plant grew with astounding quickness. It was a true, magical beanstalk. Grandfather used his cloak front like a basket, picking enough gandule pods to fill it up.

"Gandules, gandules, sweet gandules," he sang, softly. "Burtie does care for you!

"Burtie? Burtie? Where you gone to, mahn? Tis a game you playin'? I can't locate you and I must tell you some things, Burtie. I must tell you, there is a worry here, I think."

Grandfather decided to tell Burtie about the pirates somewhere about the island who had knocked him down, oh, it must've been days ago now. He didn't know why it occurred to him this morning; he might well cause Burtie to get upset. But somehow, he felt, it was important now that Burtie know, and know, too, that Jackabo had taken the gun.

Grandfather tightened his gandule cloak-basket and held it securely against him with one arm as he opened the screen into Burtie's room.

"Whew! It hot, mahn, out dah, so! Burtie! I pick lots of gandules for you to cook him."

Grandfather shuffled farther inside his old enemy's room that was still cool and still mostly shade. Burtie's bed was made neatly. The hospital sheets of faded green that Burtie had got somewhere were smooth and tight. The two pillows he used were straight up and centered against the bamboo headboard. The white, simple seersucker spread was turned down and smoothed, even to the floor. It was an elegant room in an old-fashioned, modest way. There was a long mahogany trestle table against the far wall. The table was said to have been made over a hundred years ago, when there had been mahogany trees aplenty on the island. Something was wrong about the table, Jackabo could tell. The very pretty, very old silk cloth that had covered it was missing. That was it. But there was something else. Whatever it was now lived in the land of the forgotten of Jackabo's mind. It will come back, give it time, Jackabo thought.

Slowly, Grandfather eased himself down onto the footstool by the screen door. He held tightly to the gandules.

All the years, Grandfather thought. He had grown up as a boy with young master Burten, sharing the hillside, the beaches and sea, pomegranate and mango. Even clothing they shared. And now, in these many weeks, they shared life again. But in all that long time Jackabo had never known old heathen Burtie Rawlings to make his own bed.

I make it for him, Grandfather thought grimly. I always straighten his room up, and mine, years and years. For I the black child, dontcha see. The custom of slave people, makin' the beds.

"I just a slave," Grandfather muttered bitterly. And now my master gone. Who am I? he thought. An old slave of long ago. "No. No!" he cried. Get hold yourself. We share the chores. He cook my breakfast, these weeks. "I make his bed." It's fair and even. "I fish." He cook the fish. He do plenty work. He stronger than me, can go longer.

Jackabo held himself in, held on, and looked around the room. Things were different. The yellow string rug was under the bed, crumpled up on the floor in front of the bed, out of its place. Burtie's cabinet behind the bed was open. The drawer in his end table next to where his head lay was open slightly, maybe a hand wide. It was there that Burtie kept his gun, the gun that Grandfather had taken.

Suddenly, Grandfather felt frightened. His eyes rested on the mahogany table. Something else was missing, that was what was also wrong. It came to Jackabo. Burtie kept a very beautiful silver urn on the table. It had belonged to his great-grandfather Burten, the old planter himself. Real, solid silver, it was, too. And Burtie polished it frequently against the salt air.

Old Jackabo stared at the place on the table where the urn should have been. He dropped his hands to his sides, and all the gandules tumbled from his cloak front to the floor. He gazed at the pile of them and kicked them with his sandal. The room was not right. The room was out of order.

"Burtie, Burtie. Somethin's wrong and I don't know

what to do. Where you go to, Burtie? Burtie!"

Grandfather sighed. His eyes filled with tears, but he turned them back. He would not cry. No good of that, he thought. He left Burtie's room, stumbling a bit. His legs had grown stiff from sitting still. Best to keep moving. Find some breakfast. That meant going up to the big house and then back down to the kitchen. In the big house was the refrigerator.

"Wish things were not scattered so," he said to himself. Grandfather took up his staff that stood against a tumbled-down forecourt wall. He kept to the shade of trees and bushes as, slowly, he climbed the path to the house. The hill seemed always easier for him than climbing the steep, winding, back stairs. They made him feel like some servant of old. Made him tired.

But the hill was a hard, steep climb. Perhaps too much for the old mahn. Jackabo was trembling with the exertion by the time he got up to the great house at the very height. He breathed hard and fast as he walked the wide portico around to the back of the house. There had once been a carriage road right there at the rear. But only a trace of it remained now. Grandfather stood, holding on to his staff. Here the other side of the hill did not simply go steeply down. Some twenty-five yards away from the back of the house, it plunged jaggedly toward a vast open expanse.

He leaned against one of the portico columns, bent over, catching his breath. He felt lifted, though. He felt free, being so at the top. There was a splendid silence surrounding him. Old Jackabo could see so very far. Strong breezes stirred the house, causing it to shudder and moan. They turned his sweat cool and passed coolly over his bald head. He could clearly sense that the mansion was empty. For Jackabo Rawlings could feel when Burtie was about.

Out from the sheer drop of the hillside was the expanse of land shaped like a horseshoe. At the opening of it, far off, was the gleaming Caribbean Sea. All blue-bright today was the Caribbee, with surging ocean hitting the reef out there. And after breaking, gliding in smoothly and prettily, with just a gentle surf to bubble and foam over the dark sand and volcanic rocks and pebbles of Medusa Beach.

Dah, Medusa Point, thought Grandfather. Off to the left, the Point was the headland. Ah, beauteous! He studied the great circle of sky and sea cupped in the horseshoe-shaped land. The land rose in cliffs across the expanse on the far side of the horseshoe. Some movement down there in the mesquite and heat and bush caught his eye. He thought he saw humming-birds. He did see the white cattle egrets; a few blue herons. Grandfather could make out colorful orchids on some of the near boulders. A few pelicans swooping way off in the Caribbee, fishing. And over everything was the placid stillness of faultless sky and water.

The great house was cool inside as Grandfather stepped in. The refrigerator was in the best shade in an empty room up against the hillside. Grandfather never remembered where it was exactly. He stumbled upon it while, hoping against hope, searching for Burtie anyway, in each of the dust-filled, scorpion-infested rooms. Climbing through such a big place had taken all his nerve and most of his energy. Twice he sat down on the staircase, feeling the ghosts of times gone. Things skittered and ran as he stumbled and shuffled about, watching his feet. And he found the refrigerator, at last, humming to itself in the shadows.

"Ah, good!" said Grandfather, his voice echoing. "Not so good as finding dirty Burtie, but glad to see you, too!" he told the refrigerator.

There was a plastic jug of cold water on the shelf. A quart bottle of dangerous punch. Rice and beans and the hamburger sauce left over from the night before. Lettuce, onions, tomatoes. A few wrinkled potatoes. All such food had to be kept in the refrigerator. The cereal and milk were both nice and cold.

Grandfather took them up and slammed the refrigerator closed. He hurried out and along the portico to the front door again. And with his staff in one hand now and the milk and cereal cradled in the other, he made his way down the steep slope. It was not easy; it would not do for him to stumble. It took him some time, too. All the while, he envisioned the ghostly mansion at his back.

"Yes," he told himself. "I am alone. All alone. Unless Burtie does stay in the kitchen all night. I don't think so. I will hunt him out. Maybe he does leave. If he does not be coming back by dark, I will do something."

He had no idea what. Had he forgotten something? Something, over the edge of his memory.

Always Burtie was there for him, and he and Burtie thought things out together. Now Burtie was nowhere to be found. It was a condition that Grandfather couldn't fathom. Confusion, frustration caused his eyes to fill again. Difficult to walk a path with tears blinding one's sight! And without Burtie to lead or to lean upon. At last Jackabo reached the kitchen without hurting himself. He hadn't thought he would make it this time. He went in and sat down at the long supper table. He breathed deeply; rested a moment.

Cereal and milk. He found a spoon, and a bowl from the cupboard. He sat down again.

"I forget the sugar. Pity on me!" he murmured, smiling wanly. Sugar was kept in the refrigerator as well. Too difficult to go get it in the mansion.

Hard to think clearly without his old enemy there to argue and rage, to remind him.

# Eleven

Junius walked into his house, and in short order the steady beat of his daily life changed. His father was home. Junius could smell the tempting aroma of supper that had been cooked and served. He was somewhat late. The house seemed too quiet. He hung up his coat and set down his duffel bag. He was about to call for his mother when his father came into the living room.

Junius smiled. "Hello, Fahtha," he said.

"Good evening, son," his father said. "Have a good day?"

"Yes," Junius said. "Was over studying at Sarrietta's. Got a lot done. You? Have a good day?"

"Yes," said his father, and he sat down.

Junius felt good, seeing his father, particularly after having to deal with Sarrietta's mother. It was all right for the day to end once Damius Rawlings was home from work. His father was a handsome man, Junius thought. There was no other father in the neighborhood quite so intelligent, nor quite so steady and punctual. "I am afraid of him, just a little, I think," Junius told himself.

He noticed the Christmas tree already in its stand, there by the fireplace. "Smell the pine scent!" he said. "It tis filling up this room and makin' it a forest. I guess we start decorating tonight." Junius loved the ritual of decorating the tree. He did most of it. His mother helped by finding all the old ornaments they put away carefully in boxes with tissue paper year after year. She enjoyed most throwing the tinsel on the tree. His father always strung the lights, at least three long strands of them. Then he would sit in his easy chair by the fire and direct, watching their very own Noel tree take shape.

"Junius," Mr. Rawlings said. He had a letter in his hand.

Junius turned away from the tree, smiling. His father was holding the letter out, indicating it to him.

"It's a letter from Grandfahtha, yes?" Junius said. He saw his father's expression. Junius' smile faded.

He went over to take the letter. Instead, Damius gently steered him over to the couch, where he sat down beside him.

"Something's wrong, isn't it?" Junius asked. Suddenly, his hands were trembling and he was scared inside.

"We have to remain calm, Junius," his father said.

"But I do think something might be wrong down there."
His father put a firm hand on his shoulder.

"Oh. Oh," Junius said. "I knew we should have done
something! You let him go down there all by himself."

"He did so want to go back to the Snake," his father
said. He sighed heavily. "I guess I convinced myself
nothing bad would happen to him. It was my decision
to wait and see. I'm sorry."

Junius looked up at his father. His heart was beating
so loudly, it frightened him. "Fahtha, is he . . . is
he . . ." He couldn't say the words.

"No, no, Junius, I've given you the wrong impression. Grandfather is alive, but I can't say he is well."

Junius was listening to the sound of his father's
voice.

It's an American voice, he thought, as he had so
many times. That had nothing to do with the subject
at hand. But maybe it did. Junius' father prided himself
on having no island accent. And Junius was reminded
that Grandfather Jackabo had taught him words and
had helped him learn to talk—like an island mahn, he
thought. His heart ached with good memories of
Grandfather. Oh. Oh.

"Junius. I'll have to go down there."

He stared at his father; he felt a sudden anger. "You
hate it down there," he said before he thought. But he
knew at once that it was true.

"Hate is complicated," finally, his father said. Unsmiling, he stared in front of him. "But I must go down to see that my father is all right."

"Fahtha! You have to let me go with you. Oh, please let me go, too!" Junius pleaded.

"No!" said his father. "You're not going down there. Ever."

"Can it be so awful to let me go help my own grandfahtha?" asked Junius. Sadly, he turned his head away from Damius. "You hate it so much, you must make me hate it, too!"

His father looked embarrassed, almost ashamed. "Junius, you . . . you still have school," he managed to say.

"But it tis out on Friday. When will you go? I can miss school. It tis not important." Fleetingly, he thought of Sarrietta. It stopped him a moment. But now she would have to wait. Would she wait for him? He couldn't think about that now. Something had happened to Grandfather Jackabo.

His father seemed to ponder the situation. "I'd better leave by Thursday," he said. "I've already called the airlines. Son, they are booked solid—"

"You call them back for me," Junius demanded. "Fahtha, you must let me go with you. I have to go! Grandfahtha would want me to come. Oh, please?"

"Junius—"

"Please, Fahtha. I won't be any trouble. I won't eat much, I promise."

That made his father smile, almost. But he shook his head. "It costs a lot, even for one ticket, and I have to go on standby—"

"I have money!" Junius exclaimed. "I have nine hundred dollars in my account. Remember? You can have it all!"

"But what about your schoolwork?" Damius said.

He was stalling, weakening, Junius could tell. He knew now that there was a good chance his father would let him go. "I'll get all the assignments for the rest of the week tomorrow," he said eagerly. "Not much! I can do it all on the way."

They sat close together. Junius knew he must keep talking to keep his father from changing his mind. "What's a standby?" he asked.

"It means you have no reserved seat," Damius said. "It means you have to wait for somebody to cancel their ticket so you can have their seat. It can take a long time, Junius."

"Well, I don't mind waitin'," Junius said. "Fahtha, I have never been anywhere, you know that. I have never seen where you and Grandfahtha come from. It cannot hurt to see the lands of my fahtha and grand-fahtha."

He waited in the quiet between them. His father looked down at his hands, smoothing one hand with the other, as though they ached.

"You never wanted me to see the Caribbean land," Junius said softly.

"It's more complicated than that," Damius said, sighing again.

"You keep saying that. Fahtha, I don't know what that means!" Junius said.

"Well, maybe we'll talk about it sometime."

"But not now?" Junius asked.

"No." Deep in his father's eyes there was sadness, even pain.

Junius quickly changed the subject. Keep talking, he thought. "Can Muhtha come, too, to the island?" he asked.

"She could if I could get her a seat," his father said. "But getting more than one seat at this late date might prove impossible. She won't go, in any case. Your mother doesn't like holiday crowds and she hates flying."

Junius nodded, remembering that his mother didn't like to fly. "And here I am in high school," he said, "and never have I been on an airplane. It tis a cryin' shem, dontcha know!"

"You don't have to exaggerate the accent, Junius," his father told him.

"Well, it tis the way your own fahtha speaks," Junius said, "and you don't like it." He knew he was being daring. After having dealt with Sarrietta's mother, he was feeling bold. "And please don't say it's more complicated . . . please don't say that again, Fahtha," Junius said.

"It is, Junius, but I won't say that again."

"So," Junius said. He couldn't wait any longer. "Am I goin' with you or not? Oh, please!"

Again the charged silence as his father thought about it. At last, he said, "It would be a Christmas gift if we were able to get two seats together. You might have to sit by yourself."

"I don't care. I'll surely be afraid, but I don't care!"

"All right," said his father. "But you'll see the islands are—" He paused, looked off across the room. He didn't finish the thought. "I'd better call the airlines back," he said, getting up.

"But I have some questions, Fahtha."

"Later," his father said. "Wait until your mother finds out I'm taking you with me!" He chuckled then. But it was a dry, unhappy sound.

"Will we be home before Christmas?" Junius asked.

"We'd better be, or your mother will get after me. I want to be back by next Tuesday or Wednesday. By the twentieth or the twenty-first."

"And school's out anyway for that whole week," Junius said. "It works out perfectly!"

Damius handed his son Grandfather Jackabo's letter. In all the excitement, Junius had forgotten it a moment.

"What does it say?" he wanted to know.

Damius shrugged, looking uncertain. "It appears to have been written over several days," he said. "I think the son of the planter, Burtie Rawlings, decided he'd had enough of your grandfather or the old estate, or both. It seems he's left, and Father doesn't remember him going or why. So he's made up some story—you read it. See what you make of it."

Damius took a folded piece of napkin from his pocket. It was the wrapped seashell that Grandfather Jackabo sent to Junius in every letter he mailed home. Junius took it; his father left the room.

He held the envelope up to his nose, and the napkin, too. There is was, the scent that he knew as the scent of the tropics. Sea scent, flower scent, and spice aroma. He closed his eyes and it was as if sunlight and heat filled his brain.

"I'll know what it tis really like very soon now," he murmured. Finally he read the letter, scanning sections and pausing at key phrases:

I get the boat started this very morning, so I know I can get it started. The first day after Burtie gone, I couldn't get it started. Maybe that twas because I search so long for him. So tiring, doncha know! Way up the top of this hill and down and around and all over, mahn. And so hot! But he not nowhere, oh Gawd! . . .

So to mail this I must get the boat goin. And I will take this letter by dory to over town. Do I seem also over far to you? I am also over far and alone now. See I write so you may help me know what to do. I don know what to do. I remember, take up the field glasses belong to Burtie. They are still here I use them to look way, way along, but no Burtie. Can you all help me. Now I have this thought, it come to me one mornin. Night . . . The pirates comin up here, I don see how they know where to come for me. But they don get me. They get poor Burtie. . . . They take from his room. Silver and maybe his money. Burtie try to find his gun. But I have the gun in the boat. I take it awhile ago. . . . Oh, Gawd! Burtie gone. The pirates take him. I remember, come back slowly, I think it a dream.

See Burtie hangin down the back of a pirate. They take him off. He sound asleep down one of them's back. Or maybe they hurt him and he dead.

I find the gandules just today. Haven't been back to Burtie's until today. They not all rotten. A little dusty. I will cook them what tis not rotten, then maybe Burtie come on back home.

"Oh, Grandfahtha!" Junius whispered. "Don't get hurt on that hillside. Don't drown off that boat!"

He wondered what gandules were. Grandfather hadn't explained. They were a food, perhaps, and they could rot. Junius finished the letter. *Please help me find my old enemy*, it said at the end. Grandfather wouldn't shoot anybody, would he? He hadn't shot old Burtie Rawlings and forgotten? Junius wondered.

Junius closed his eyes a moment. No. No. He would never believe Grandfather could do something like hurting someone. But what was it, pirates again! He had never known Grandfather to make up things. But then, he didn't know how much Grandfather might have changed, grown old, so far away from his loved ones.

It's all our fault, thought Junius, a forlorn feeling in his heart. We should not have let him go so, so *over far*, himself. Grandfahtha Jackabo meant to go back there to die, I think. He think he's gettin' too old and maybe we don't want him! Oh, I know that's why he would leave me. That's the only reason he would leave me! Why didn't I think of that before!

He sighed. He took up the napkin and carefully opened it. There were the tiny pieces of shell, like cookie crumbs. He closed it agan. He would put it with the other napkins he had received from Grand-father Jackabo.

There was no way for Junius to tell precisely when Grandfather had written the letter, for he seemed to have added to it over a period of days. There were three places he seemed to start the letter, writing *Junius son*, *Damius my son my own boy*, and *Daughterinlaw Jaylene* again. Or maybe Grandfather had added to the letter many times during one day—Junius didn't know.

Given the mails from the islands, Junius thought. And considering that Grandfather never put a date on one of his letters, well. It could be more than a week now that Burtie Rawlings has gone away.

"Yes, Fahtha and I must go," he whispered. "We must truly go there." Oh, what will it be like? he wondered. What will we find? Grandfather will be all right, I know he will. But an island! Do we fly to it? What is it like, with so much water around, swimming beaches? Leatherback turtles! Oh, I can *taste* it, I can taste the *Caribbee*, I can!

Junius went to his room. He put the letter in his

desk drawer, where he kept the other letters and the shell napkins. Then he lay down on his bed. He didn't listen to Jimi Hendrix this time. His mother would be in, soon, to call him to supper. He just lay there, looking over at the dark, still world of Grandfather Jackabo's great globe. He did not get up to plug it in and see it glow.

A tiny dot, I am, he thought. Tinier than an island dot. A tiny me on a big world. Don't get separated from Fahtha. No tellin' where you might end up. I know nothing atall about travelin'.

"Junius. Supper." His mother opened the door just as he was dozing. She didn't come in. "Wake up," she said. "Your supper will dry up if you don't eat it up soon."

"I'm not asleep," he murmured sleepily. He sat up.

"I hear you're going," she said.

He remembered and smiled. Nodded. "I'm going," he said.

"Well, I don't know what to think," Jaylene said.

"Did Fahtha get me a ticket?"

"Yes," she said. "But it's on standby. You were lucky. There're lots of planes at Christmas. But we don't know how many standbys will be ahead of you."

Junius didn't understand about that. He didn't want to know. "Just so we can get there," he said.

"You'll get there," his mother said, "but it might take a day."

"A whole day?" he said.

"You'll wait at the airport for as long as it takes."

"And then how long will it take, once we are on the plane?"

"An hour and a half to Atlanta. That part is already reserved. But then at least a three-hour wait," Jaylene said.

"Three hours!"

"Junius, it's not easy to make connections. That's only how long you'll wait if you can get on the first plane that's going—if not, you'll wait much longer. Wait until you see."

"I am dying to see," he said. "Then what?"

"Then a few more hours. Your father knows better than I do. Let him tell you the rest. I don't want to think about it."

"Muhtha, are you angry at us for going?" he asked her.

"No, I'm not angry. It's just that, well, I know it's selfish of me. But I had our Christmas all planned. Damius would be home for the holidays, using some of his vacation time, and we would go to movies over vacation. We'd go out to dinner—"

"But we plan to be back before Christmas, Muhtha," Junius said. "We'll have time to do all that."

She didn't say anything; she looked as if she didn't quite believe it.

Junius followed his mother to the kitchen, where he would have his supper. He felt nervous from excitement. There was a worry, one that came to him while he was dozing, that he could not share with his parents.

Sarrietta Dobbs was there in his thoughts with Grandfather Jackabo and his trouble. There was a worry with her that he needed to think about.

Who would tutor her while he was gone? But it will be vacation time soon, he thought. Nobody work much over vacation. But some teachers were sure to give homework. It wasn't fair, but the G-O teacher always seemed to delight in giving homework over holidays. And Sarrietta would not have him to help her much. But I can help her when I get back. Yes. It will work out. It will be fine. Junius, why you have to worry so? She's your girl. Maybe you won't lose her that quickly. He tried not to think about the expression "Out of sight, out of mind."

He ate his supper. "What clothes will I take?" he asked his mother, who was still in and out of the kitchen. She liked a cup of tea after supper.

"I'll look through your summer things," she said, sitting down next to him.

"But it's cold out," he said.

"Well, not where you're going," said his father. He came in to have a cup of tea, too. "You won't need a lot."

"Will you help me pack?" he asked his mother and father.

"Junius, it will only take a minute," said his mother.

"Okay, if you say so," he said. "Oh, it's getting very excitin'!"

The next day, in school, he told Sarrietta that he and his father had to go to see about Grandfather Jackabo. He tried to sound casual about it. But there was little time to chat between classes. Maybe I should wait until after school, he thought. "I can't study with you tonight," he told Sarrietta. "I must pack my things tonight."

Sarrietta looked upset. "Junius. Well, you get to travel. Merry Christmas!" she said. She turned away from him. Looking over her shoulder back at him. He felt she would have said more but she had to hurry, and he had no time to soothe her. He wished she had shown sympathy for his Grandfather Jackabo. He thought Sarrietta always looked so beautiful. And now she also looked very angry.

# Twelve

Junius paid for his own plane ticket. What a lot of money it cost! A little more than six hundred dollars. But he had insisted to his father. "I want to," he said. "I want to go, but I will not go unless I pay my own way."

Damius Rawlings had looked proudly at his son. Junius had three hundred dollars left. He had withdrawn an extra hundred Wednesday from his bank account.

"I want to find presents for Grandfahtha and for Muhtha and Sarrietta."

"A hundred dollars should do it," his father said.

"Well, some of it will be travelin' money for me, too," he said. "I already buy your present, Fahtha," Junius added shyly.

"You do plan ahead," his father said.

Junius felt close to his father, closer than usual, and the feeling was wonderful. He also felt free, for he was out of school and on holiday before all of the other students were. By Wednesday afternoon all the students knew that he was going to the Caribbean Islands, that he would swim in warm ocean while they froze to death in the cold. The news had traveled like wildfire. Junius had to laugh out loud several times. How good to be the son of an island mahn! His heart fairly beat to a calypso rhythm.

But there was the one worry. Sarrietta. He had thought to call her last night. She would talk to him only for a minute over the phone.

"Our plane leaves the first thing in the mornin'," he told her. "I wonder if I might come over now, just for a little time, yes? I have more time than I thought."

"No," she had said. Then she had softened it by saying, "I thought you had to pack."

"I already pack," he said. "It takes no time atall to pack for the islands, see?"

"Oh, the islands! That's all you talk about."

"Sarrietta, don't be angry."

"Who's angry?" she said. "Listen, I have to go, it's too late for you to come over."

"Sarrietta, it's only nine o'clock."

"Mother wouldn't like it," she said. "I'm sorry."

"Muhtha don't like me, you mean," he answered back.

"Junius, I hope your grandfather's all right. I have to go. Send me a postcard."

"Maybe I'll send you a letter," he told her.

"Merry Christmas. 'Bye." And she had hung up before he could remind her he would be back before Christmas.

Now it was the very morning of departure, and Mrs. Rawlings drove her husband and Junius to the airport. Junius' alarm had gone off at five thirty. They had to leave at six thirty in the dark in order to get to the airport an hour ahead of time. "You never know how long the lines can be at Christmastime," his father had told Junius.

Junius felt nervous, shaky, from getting up so early. He thought he might become sick somewhere along the way. He was tired; he hadn't slept much last night because of his confused thoughts about Sarrietta. She was angry with him and he loved her so, with no chance to tell her. He'd also thought long and hard about Grandfather Jackabo. Finally, he couldn't sort any of it out and had fallen asleep.

Junius wore only a lightweight jacket that he could stuff into his duffel bag when the climate changed from cold to hot. In the duffel bag were the few clothes his father and mother had said he would need. A pair of dress pants that he would wear at the hotel they would stay at tonight. A hotel! On the big island, his father had said. "But why we must stay at a hotel?" Junius had asked.

"You'll see," said his father. "You don't want to know everything at once, do you, and not have surprises?" Junius said he guessed not, but he wasn't sure.

So much change in just a few days! He couldn't take it all in.

He had shorts and swimming trunks and blue jeans besides the ones he wore now with a good shirt. He had T-shirts and one or two more other shirts in the duffel, as well as his AM/FM stereo cassette player and headphones. And a small, flat Instamatic camera. He had two of his best Jimi Hendrix tapes. He had one cassette of Joan Armatrading, who was a singer from the islands. Junius had taped her from the radio and thought her West Indian vocals might be good to listen to on Snake Island. He had brought blank tapes with him as well, to tape whatever island music he heard broadcast. He decided on not taking any schoolbooks with him. There would be time for study when he got back.

They rode out of town in the dark. But by the time they reached the airport, it was getting light. The airport was like another world, brightly lighted and sprawling over the frozen countryside, as if nobody ever slept.

Then time seemed to speed. Damius Rawlings stood in a long line. The line moved slowly. Finally, he was getting their seat assignments.

"I thought it was standby for a plane," Junius said. He stood off to the side with his mother. He was fidgeting, getting tired. His duffel rested at his feet. He would take it on the plane with him.

"You buy the tickets," his mother explained. "And

you do wait for a plane that has cancellations. Only on this leg of the trip, you don't have to wait. There was room on an early flight to Atlanta. So now you have reserved seats that far, at least."

Junius remembered—his father had said that they would change planes in Atlanta and take a jumbo jet to the big island. "You'll like it, Junius," Mr. Rawlings had said. "You won't believe how it can lift off the ground, it's so big."

Soon they were saying good-bye to his mother. He and his father hugged her and spoke their farewells. "Wish you were going too!" Junius told her.

"I can get my Christmas presents bought and wrapped without you peeking," she told him, and that made him laugh. He loved to see presents under the Noel tree.

They went through security. He and his father walked down a passage to the plane gate. No time even to look back, to wave.

"It takes so much doing to get started," he said, and added, "Will Grandfahtha be all right, you think?"

"It doesn't help to worry," his father said.

"I know," he murmured under his breath, "but it makes me feel better, dontcha see!"

They were shuffling aboard. Junius' heart was going fast. He thought of Sarrietta with a lonely feeling. He couldn't believe all this was happening. The sound of plane engines. As he stepped onto the plane, he saw the pilot to his left through a door in a very small space with instruments all around. Seeing that cramped quarters gave Junius a fright.

From that little space he drives this big plane? he thought.

A uniformed host took his ticket and a part of his boarding pass and gave the rest back to him. He put it in his shirt pocket, as he'd seen his father do.

"You sit by the window, son," his father said. Junius climbed in. They had two seats together near the wing. Junius had a sinking feeling when he thought about how those thin wings would keep them in the air. And the motor and all those instruments, all the people, too.

It didn't take long. Soon he had his first plane flight. The day was clear, with the crisp, sunny distance of winter all the way to Atlanta.

"First-time travelers always get the good flights," his father said.

"There are bad flights?" Junius said, looking alarmed.

"I mean the weather," Mr. Rawlings said. "Good weather makes for a good, smooth flight."

"It doesn't feel like we are movin' atall," Junius said.

They went over brown mountains. He followed their route on a map the airline provided. He was served breakfast while he looked out the window. It was a wonderful breakfast—an omelette and bacon. Fruit and coffee cake. Afterward, he leaned back, but he couldn't sleep. His father was sleeping soundly. People all around were going to sleep, or were reading.

Just as if they are in their own homes, Junius thought. How can they sleep in front of everybody like that?

He watched the plane wing out his window. He knew the plane was going very fast; they were up more than thirty thousand feet, about five and a half miles up. It was a long way down. You could see tiny things down there. Tiny, shiny things, winking in the sunlight. Tiny lakes, ribbons of rivers curving, snaking.

Snake Island. Junius closed his eyes, finally, for they felt strained. He was suspended somewhere between wakefulness and sleep, with the single, monotonous tone of the engines ever present in his thoughts of Grandfather, of sea and Sarrietta, school, holidays.

The next thing he knew, they were coming down. They were in the Atlanta area, the steward said. Junius looked out to see a hilly countryside and bright orangish-red soil. Suburbs, many houses. Twenty minutes later, they were walking off the plane.

The long wait began. "Even when you are impatient," Junius told himself during the hours, "time does pass. It does go. Nothing will stop it goin'. You just do go with it and it does go more quickly."

He walked around. He bought magazines. He played pinball. He always came back to where his father was seated in a central area near their gate. They finally went to lunch. They rode a moving sidewalk to get there. It didn't surprise him. You stood and the thing moved steadily a long, long way along. Now that he had flown, nothing could surprise him.

They waited four hours for a plane. No room on the plane they had hoped to get on. An hour later, they got on one. They had to sit apart. His father was way off in the smoking section. But they were lucky. People who didn't want to smoke were exchanging seats with people who did want to smoke. Not long, and Junius and his father had two seats, one by the window.

"I think you bring us luck," Mr. Rawlings told him. "It's warm back there with the smokers."

"Planes are like houses?" Junius joked. "Warm upstairs, cold downstairs?"

"Make yourself right at home," his father joked back.

Everybody goin' somewhere, like me, Junius thought. Don't ever try to figure out how this plane stay up or it might fall down.

The plane was enormous, and it was full of people, every seat taken.

It tis magic! He felt his insides strumming with excitement.

When at last they were up over the ocean, they picked up heavy clouds for a long way. But a third of the way through the flight, the air cleared and the bluest, most beautiful sea presented itself. Turquoise and silver and white, he thought. Not a cold blue of winter sky, but a summer, deep blue, an azure blue of ocean that was warm and tropic. Little green-and-blue islands were strewn like toys in the water. Bigger than on Grandfather's globe, they had the same yellow edges, lines of sand. Junius took out his camera and carefully snapped the shutter out the window.

They were served a meal. Junius was not hungry when he began, but soon he had an appetite. Baked chicken with a sauce that was good and hot. Delicious.

"I thought there would be a movie," he said afterward.

"Not this time," his father said. "Maybe on the way home."

He studied the map. He knew the names of the islands far below before the pilot announced what they were.

"Turks and Caicos islands," the pilot was saying, but Junius already knew.

"We're still some way away," he told his father.

And later on, "Hispaniola is out the windows on the right side," the pilot told them.

"We're getting there!" Junius told his father.

"It is beautiful there," his father said, somewhat wistfully.

"I don't see Snake Island on this map," Junius said.

"Too small," his father said.

Not nice, Junius thought, just because you are small, you and Grandfahtha, to leave you out.

"Is that why you don't like the Snake, because it tis so small?" Junius asked him. He knew better, but he wanted to talk about it.

His father looked at him.

"Is that question too complicated, too?" Junius said.

He felt relaxed now. It was as if he had grown up into someone older in the space of a plane trip. He felt confident; after all, he had a girlfriend. He had dealt with her mother.

His father studied him, as though seeing him in a new light. "Sometimes," he began, "there are too many memories, good and bad." Then he paused. Junius thought he had stopped talking, but he said, "The Snake was one place I lived; I had many homes. We went island hopping, my father and I."

"You did not like the Snake, then?" Junius said.

Mr. Rawlings shook his head. "It was too small, too stifling. A set place for everyone to stay."

"What do you mean?" Junius said.

"Well, you couldn't exchange your place for another place," his father said. "No mobility. You were all your life what you were born. . . ." Abruptly, he stopped and did not start again. The sound of the plane engines droned. Junius had come close to his father to hear. Now he leaned back.

Fahtha tells, and he doesn't tell, Junius thought. And what mahn wasn't what he was born?

They landed in coming darkness and in a tropic, blowing rain. Junius could see streaks of orange and red along the horizon, where the sun had gone down. The plane seemed to shudder as wind hit it. The wings swayed and Junius covered his eyes. They landed hard. People applauded. Swift rain hit the plane windows. By the time they taxied in, the rain had stopped, the darkness of clouds lifted and night held off. But lights were on everywhere. There were palm trees lining the airport perimeter. The palms were wildly waving, leaning to one side. Next, they were shuffling off the plane. It took a long time, with so many people. More than two hundred people.

They found their way through the busy airport. Junius moved like a sleepwalker; but he observed everything. He heard all sorts of languages and rhythms. People looked exotically different. There were all kinds of people. All colors of people, black, brown, tan, and white. The majority of people were shades of brown. Perhaps they were all island people. People who came to islands or lived on islands seemed suddenly different from other people.

I am two and a half thousand miles from home, he thought. He felt like a world traveler and a bit smug about it, too.

Wish Sarrietta could be here. That would be perfect! I've seen no one here as pretty as she.

They took a taxi to their hotel, The Caribbean. When they got there, Junius found it a very large, modern place. Many tourists.

"It's your last chance for a decent shower," his father told him.

"Really?" said Junius. "Is the Snake so primitive?"

"It won't have changed much. Things are harder, life is harder on a small island. I don't know what it will be like where we'll be staying," Mr. Rawlings said.

"We're stayin' with Grandfahtha," Junius said.

"On a ruined plantation," his father added. He looked uneasy.

"Don't worry, Fahtha," Junius told him. "Grandfahtha able to live there, so we too able to live there."

It was good and dark outside now. The hotel was an open place; the tropic breezes came right in and rustled flowers and plantings that were all around, making a pleasant sound.

Two tired travelin' mahns through travelin' for the night, Junius thought. Something inside him he'd held on to tightly for the whole trip now eased up.

Home safe! Relax. It do feel like home. I mean, I don't feel like a stranger here. Feel just like I belong, Junius thought.

They had a room on the sixteenth floor. Air conditioned. Junius had to see everything. He went out on the balcony to stand a moment. The wind was high and hot. It was a long way down. The hotel grounds were well lit. There were exotic land birds, swans and flamingos, walking about. Some had already nested for the night. He could hear the ocean and he could almost see its dark shape way off. Parading along every path, outlining the beaches, were the wildly swaying palm trees. This was truly a different place, the tropics.

It was too hot out. In a moment Junius' skin felt clammy and sticky. He went back inside.

Mr. Rawlings was stretched out on the bed. "Better

get some sleep," he said. "The ferry to the Snake is on the other side of this island. And we start out first thing in the morning."

"I'm too excited to sleep," Junius told him. He hadn't realized how really excited he was until just now.

"Well, rest, then. I know I'm exhausted," his father said.

Junius looked at everything in the room. Even the furniture was different down here. They had two double beds with brilliant green-and-yellow spreads. The headboards and footboards of the beds were bamboo. Brightly cushioned chairs had bamboo frames. The room had a couch, a large bathroom. Everything was made lighter, brighter, to fit in with tropic life.

"Your mother and I stayed here years ago when we came here on a trip," Mr. Rawlings said. He had been watching Junius look around.

"I thought this place was brand-new," Junius said.

"No, but it's fairly new for a hotel. Maybe twenty, twenty-five years old. That's not old," his father said.

"However, your mother and I didn't go to Snake Island," his father continued. "Father wasn't there then. We changed planes here, to a smaller plane. He had gone back to an island called Nevis, where I was born, which I liked better. That's where your mother and I were going."

"I didn't know all that," Junius said. He sat down on his bed. He hadn't realized how tired he was until he was off his feet. Soon he took off his shoes and put his feet up. He was lying comfortably back against the pillows. "I didn't know Muhtha had been down here. Come to think of it, I never knew much about your life down here."

His father was silent a long moment. It was clear that the islands were not his favorite topic. But perhaps in the space between the beds, somewhere between father and son, the formality had melted somewhat.

"Well, your mother and I made our lives in the States, where she was born. There was no time for me to look back," his father said. "You were young— your grandfather told you many things. We talked about the islands, but you probably have forgotten. You grew out of childhood and had other interests."

Not really, thought Junius. My interests always were Grandfahtha's, too.

"It was nothing so great, living in the islands," his father went on. "I guess I felt deprived down here. I know I did. I was ambitious and we were poor.

"Junius."

"Yes, Fahtha?"

His father stared at the ceiling. His eyelashes fluttered. And then Damius fell quietly to sleep.

For a long time Junius watched him. What were you going to say? he wondered. But now he was almost too tired and sleepy to care.

Fahtha will sleep in his clothes, he thought. So will

I. He closed his eyes. Change into fresh cooler clothes in the marnin'. He felt himself relax. Be on our merry way.

In a moment he was gone too. Sound asleep.

# Thirteen

Grandfather Jackabo no longer said his old enemy's name. Not out loud and not in his mind. When he thought of the white Rawlings, he thought of him as My Old Enemy, nothing more. It did not mean that he would not care to have the mahn back. It meant simply that the old friend was gone, perhaps forever. The buccaneers, the pirates had this mahn. What was left behind in the shadows of Jackabo's memory was the foe.

He waited patiently. Grandfather Jackabo had nothing else to do beyond his simple chores. He thought twice, three times now, before going out on the bay in the dory. He did not fish far from shore, and if he caught nothing, that was fine. But he would never go so far that he couldn't get back to land by swimming and floating. Supposing the motor died and no one was on shore to help him out of the situation? So he always took food with him, whether he would stay out at lunchtime or not. If he got stuck, he would eat the food, wait awhile, and then have strength in case he must swim home. He had no paddles for the boat.

The motor did not die. Still, he went out in the dory only twice. He missed his long afternoons on the water, eating, drinking the Planter's Punch. But it was too much for an old man to bring in the boat by himself. The Punch lost its glory when there was no one to drink with in the evening.

After two days of being by himself, Grandfather stopped drinking Planter's Punch altogether. Gradually, he felt better and he spent some time thinking out a shopping list. Another day, and he had memorized the list. He planned how he would get in the boat and go all the way to over town wharf. There, taking his time, concentrating, he would cut the engine just right and glide in and tie up the boat. And he would make his way to the grocery.

Yes, planning does be a very good thing, he thought. I plan to buy the supplies. I will buy beans and rice, canned goods, bread. Meat and vegetables, yes. I will buy me coffee. I buy English tea that steam and clear my brain.

Grandfather Jackabo no longer knew how many days had passed since he first thought of making his shopping list. He knew it must be time to go into town again. He had gone once to mail a letter. But he feared going so far away from the hillside of Rawlings. Supposing Damius should come and find him gone? True, Damius must go through over town in order to take the coast road to the hillside. But over town had many streets, and it was easy to miss somebody you might be looking for.

Now Grandfather marked time by thinking, "a few days ago" such and such happened. "A few days from now" I must do this or that. Nothing happened and there was little to do.

So he waited. He didn't know how many days it had been since his old enemy had disappeared. He thought it days ago that he had written to his Damius over far in America and to Junius son. His days were confusing. They were very long when they passed without him taking much notice. He knew how to conserve his strength. He ate as little as possible, in order to save what small amount of food he had left. His supper consisted of rice and beans and hard, stale bread that had gone moldy, coffee. He cut away the mold from the bread. He drank his coffee black, since he had run out of milk. For breakfast he had dry cereal with a mango sliced on top. It was good, and there were plenty of mangoes in the cultivated area that his old enemy had taken care of over the years. There was a grapefruit tree there, but the fruit wasn't ripe now. Imagine his delight when he recalled the cultivated area, which was to the right around the hill away from the kitchen. He didn't see it all the time and so he hadn't remembered it. But a few days ago he had, and he collected ripe mangoes right away.

There were the gandules growing aplenty, but he

was saving them in case his old enemy returned. Grandfather came to believe that if he stopped moving entirely, he would not need to eat. One whole day he did not move but once or twice. He still got hungry and had to eat. He also got weak. Then he forgot what he had come to believe and went back to doing and eating as before.

A few days ago he thought somebody had come. He had waited so long, day after day, that he had grown lazy with waiting. He had gone deeply asleep and had grown alert when he thought he heard a voice. Maybe it had been a dream. He had pulled a chair outside by the gandules. There on the path he could see for miles. He sat there, and had fallen asleep with his coffee cup and a sliced mango in his lap.

Grandfather had opened his eyes. There before him a mahn stood. A big mahn, who seemed to glow in the light. He wore bright dress clothing, a uniform. Bright gold epaulets ornamenting the shoulders of the outfit. A hat with a shiny, black visor and gold braid. A soft voice speaking.

Grandfather listened. Perhaps this was a pirate captain. He felt fear and dreamed of buccaneers. "You've come, have you? Weyl," he murmured bravely.

Smiling mahn, speaking softly. "Jus checkan', Suh. Ya dowan ulra dah, mahn?"

Grandfather nodded. He understood. Island lands flowed in his dreams on the stranger's lilting Caribbee accent.

"Heah ya have com-*pany* co-min' sun?"

Again Grandfather Jackabo nodded, showing his fine teeth.

"Weyl, ya nee som-than', Suh, ya letus nuw."

Smiling mahn, Grandfather Jackabo, smiling back. Brothers under the sun.

And sleeping. When he awoke, there was no mahn, it had not happened. The memory joined the shadows of his forgetfulness. But he would recall a lilting voice now, whenever he thought of pirates.

The waiting became a longing. Grandfather needed voices, a helping hand, friendship. He longed, ached, for his kinfolk. At night he slept with his pillow clutched in his arms. He walked about some, at night. Never far. But the house brooding there at the top of the hill woke him with its presence. He would get up and go out to the forecourt, where he could look up. The moon hung there over the headland. He thought there were lights in the house as there had been of old. He thought there was a carnival ball going on.

Did My Old Enemy ask me to serve? he wondered. I forget. I refuse to go and be his slave. Tell him when I see him, too.

So it was Grandfather spent his days. Asleep right after dark, he was up for good and true with the morning light. Roosters crowing around the island. Mostly, he sat and waited and watched the bay. So magnificent was his view, his hills and cliffs, his cove and the deep bay with rarely a boat passing. All bathed in the spotlight of the sun. All his as he saw them. His days were long, serene, full of living dreams. He sat in his chair on the path below the kitchen, watching. Sometimes now he forgot to eat, so full was he with his days of glorious sunlight and sea sound. He didn't mind the mimis, even, those biting sandflies. He called all biting, flying insects mimis. They bit at him and they were simply another part of his days.

One day old Jackabo recalled the taste of cheese. He thought he would like some cheese with freshly baked bread, but he did nothing about it. He hadn't the strength. He did not go every morning to the kitchen, or to the refrigerator. Sometimes he got up and simply went to his chair on the path. Now it stayed in place on the path all night and all day. Some nights Grandfather got up and sat in the chair in the moonlight. He would look behind him up the hill at the great house. At last he would remember that yellow spiders liked the dark. He imagined them crawling ever nearer to spin their webs about him. And quickly he went back to bed.

One day he sat on the path and he was asleep. He was dreaming, going fast on the bay. At first he thought he rode Nulio, the great leatherback turtle. But then he heard his motor and knew he was in the dory. It seemed that Nulio was in the dory also, for they talked awhile. Then Nulio leaped overboard and the dory rode higher in the water. And Grandfather Jackabo fairly skimmed from one side of the deep bay to the other. Nobody was around, just some brown boobies in the mangroves, just him and the sound of his motor and Nulio, way deep beneath the waters, listening. Grandfather found himself listening, also, but to his memories. The motor struggled and sputtered and struggled again, urgently. And Grandfather Jackabo awoke.

He was startled for a moment to find himself on land and not the bay. He was confused that he sat so high up, but then he remembered the hillside and the chair under him. His dream had been so vivid with sight and sound. The struggling sputter he had dreamed was a boat motor appeared to be a jeep coming around the coast road. A small, snappy-looking yellow jeep.

Grandfather Jackabo did not move his head away from the coast road and the toylike automobile. The jeep struggled so because the coast road was muddy. It had rained healthily in the night. Wonderful sound of smacking rain hitting the roof and rushing down the rain troughs into the cistern. Grandfather remembered, he had heard the rain and had not walked out to sit on the hillside. He slept well, although he had felt hunger. He remembered now, he'd forgotten to eat supper. That was why his stomach had gnawed at him.

I must remember food, he thought, watching the jeep make its slow progress. Where was it going? Seeing movement brought back his longing for company. What day be this? Suddenly the date seemed important.

Christmas? Gone? No, not yet. Just a few days ago, I write my boy and his son. I write . . .

Grandfather leaned forward, watching, peering as the jeep was about to disappear down an incline. His view would be blocked in a moment by mangroves of Pelican Cove, and he would not see the jeep again until it was on the far side of the hill, below the big house. He would have to climb to the top of the hill if he wished to see it after it disappeared. Was the big house its destination, along the ancient road for coaches and horses that forked from the coast road? Grandfather Jackabo squinted, shielding his eyes. He made out two, three people, he wasn't sure how many. Two dark figures in the front, somebody, something or things in the back. Who? Should he go down?

A feeling came to him. Slowly he recalled how it felt to want and to hope. He felt expectation, that what he wanted so desperately would happen. He got up unsteadily. His legs felt as light as air. Grandfather Jackabo almost fell before he caught himself, holding on to the chair. Then he felt the heat, pressing against his temples. It made his heart beat fast, *thumpa-thumpa-thumpa*. Then the beat leaped. It took off, fluttering like a bird.

"Where my pole?" Grandfather meant his staff that he leaned on. He looked around him and found it to one side of the path. Bending was a shame. Bending took his breath, made him dizzy before he straightened. Hearing his own speaking voice, his own moan-

ing and groaning, he recognized the silence that had
been. The whole sweep of nature that had been his,
a quiet offering each and every day. Should he give it
up for the struggling sputter?

"Get me down, get me down!" Grandfather fought
with his legs, his last strength to get quickly down the
half of a hill to the bottom. He thought of rolling
down—it would be quicker. But he might hurt himself
that way. He could still hear the jeep. If he hurried,
he could go along the bottom of the hill to the fence
and the gate. Get there about the same time as the jeep
would get there.

"Move!" He spoke to his legs. He hollered at his
staff. "Move, pole! Dontcha see, it could be my Damius and Junius son. It could be. It must be!"

Grandfather giggled. He was going to make it before
the auto passed him by. He thought surely he would
make it. He was at the bottom of the hill, making his
way along the path out to the coast road. High guinea
grass on either side of him. Trees all along the way,
dwarfing him. He was laughing now, in a high whinny
of excitement. He coughed, weaving unsteadily through
the grasses. Hunger was a presence, walking with him.
He had a headache. It felt as if a film covered his sight
every other step.

Silence closed in on him. "Huh?" Grandfather said.
The motor had stopped. He rushed flatfooted as fast
as he could toward the coast road.

"Who is comin'! Who has gone! Where are you,

friend or foe? Is it My Old Enemy? Is it? Who! Who! Oh, Gawd, who?"

Grandfather was there, and he stopped in the hot and steaming damp at the sight before him. Suddenly, tears streamed down his dirt-streaked face. He was hoping so, crying so, that he could not see. Confusion, dread made him tremble. Grandfather closed his eyes. He leaned heavily on his staff, and would not dare to dream. He folded his hands in prayer.

# Fourteen

They drove a rented jeep on a divided highway. It was early morning. By seven o'clock they had checked out of the hotel. The ferry was to leave in a couple of hours, and Damius Rawlings had called ahead to reserve space for the jeep. Junius was a bit surprised that a jeep could fit on a ferry. His idea of a ferry was on the order of a large raft.

"It can carry a number of cars, a big eighteen-wheeler, and a couple of regular-sized trucks, too," his father told him.

"Really?" Junius said. He'd never been on any boat that large.

He wasn't quite awake yet. He'd eaten a sweet roll and had drunk a container of orange juice as they drove. His father had coffee and a corn muffin. He had a half dozen corn muffins in a white sack, and offered one to Junius.

"You'll need a substantial amount in your stomach

for the boat ride," his father said. "There can be high swells going over."

Junius wasn't sure what swells were like, but he would find out soon enough. He ate the corn muffin.

He'd slept hard the night before. Junius couldn't say that he had rested well. But when he woke up, the clothes he'd slept in had hardly a wrinkle. He had changed into shorts and a short-sleeved cotton shirt, comfortable clothing for the amazing heat. Already at seven o'clock the temperature had been eighty-five degrees. Now, riding along, it had to be even hotter. The breeze blowing in was hot. The sun burned him if he put his arm out the window.

Junius felt excited. The landscape looked so different from what he was used to that he thought he might be dreaming. There were enormous mountains in a blue mist at a distance from them, beyond green valleys and hills.

"Do we go through those mountains?" he asked his father.

"No, we go around them. And we go beyond them, through the foothills and beyond, to the east coast."

"Oh, I see," Junius said. "Is it a long ride?"

"About an hour, hour and a half."

"This is a very big island, then," Junius said.

"About two hundred miles long," his father said. "And some of the miles are very rugged. But we won't travel nearly the entire length."

Junius gazed at giant stands of bamboo trees. In front

of the bamboo along the highway, people had placed market tables. They sold fruits, vegetables, rugs, coconuts, even small flowering trees. They sold all kinds of water and beach playthings. There were trucks with their tailgates down and full of figs and mangoes. There were carts with bunches of large, green bananas.

"I like this," Junius said. "I like havin' people sell their goods right out in the open."

"People are poor," his father said. "What you see is all they have."

Junius didn't know if he believed that. Maybe they made a lot of money selling along the highway. He watched, but he saw no cars stop. Maybe the people *were* poor. Off the highway, beyond bamboo and bright flowers, he happened to glance into a half-hidden valley of gnarled trees and tall grasses. There he saw a whole village of shacks where people obviously lived.

"Look," he said, pointing.

His father looked once and grimly kept his eyes on the road, saying, "I don't like to see people so poor."

"Why don't they find jobs?" Junius asked.

"Oh, that's a long story, not an easy one," his father said. "There aren't enough jobs. Tourism is the industry here. Most everything else is imported."

Junius hadn't known that. "It doesn't seem right," he said. "The island should find a good industry and export what they make, and make a lot of money."

"Easier said than done," his father said. "Some businesses survive. But employment depends almost wholly on tourism. What there is to sell is mostly sun and sea."

Suddenly it rained hard. Junius hadn't noticed any clouds. What he saw above appeared to be only dark mist. But it was a soaking rain coming down. The jeep went through standing water that sprayed up as high as the hood. They both got wet. In a short while the rain stopped and the sun came out. Their clothing dried quickly.

Over everything was the heat.

"Feels like it tis hotter now, after the rain," Junius said.

"Yes, it's always like that," his father said. "There's rain, but never enough."

Even with the jeep windows open, the heat was damp, smothering. Junius felt it as if it were something alive, trying to take his breath away. It made him tired, as though he'd eaten too much breakfast. He was thirsty. Perspiration soaked him through. His face was wet. He leaned his head back and fell asleep, just like that.

An hour later they were in a coastal town, going through it to the docks. Junius awoke with a start as they traveled along narrow streets.

"You've come to," said his father.

"Yes," Junius said. "I didn't mean to go to sleep. Where are we?"

"The east coast," said his father. "This town is called Williamson."

"Williamson," Junius repeated.

The houses were painted blue and yellow and pink. They were small houses, not a foot away from the sidewalk. Doors were wide open to the street. Junius could see right inside.

"Fahtha, was it like this when you were my age?" Junius thought to ask.

People sat, watching. Over everything was the scent of salt sea.

"Not much changes," Damius said.

"Were the houses always such pretty colors?"

"Oh, yes," his father said. "All through the tropics, you find the colors."

At dockside Junius saw a ferryboat for the first time. It was large; white, orange, and black; and very sleek. It could carry fifty people, and cars, too.

"I thought ferries were little boats. . . . I don't know what I thought," Junius said.

His father nodded. "It's a pleasant way to travel," he said.

From the docks Junius had his first view of an expanse of blue water indenting the shoreline. Beyond the expanse was the far horizon. "Open sea!" he said, gazing clear away.

Damius followed his gaze. He squinted. "It is open sea," he said. "There isn't any sea quite as beautiful as the Caribbean, not to me."

"Do you miss seein' it, Fahtha?" Junius asked.

"I suppose I do."

"How is it possible you could stay away from it!"

"There wasn't anything here for me, son," Damius said.

"But it tis your home," Junius said.

His father only shook his head.

Cars lined up to get on the ferry. They parked the jeep and his father went to the Port Authority to see about the car reservation. Junius watched everything going on. All kinds of people carried everything imaginable, waiting to get on the ferry. There were backpacking young people who seemed to be in a group with two teachers. There were young men and women with scuba-diving equipment and oxygen tanks that they handled with care. People had tents packed in small cases. They carried coolers of soft drinks and food. There were mothers and babies, grandmothers, fathers, brothers, and sisters, all going from the big island to smaller islands. Some took new beach chairs wrapped in plastic with them. Junius heard various languages.

A huge truck was the first vehicle to get on the ferry. It backed on. It seemed to take up all the deck space. But no, two cars in line slowly backed on behind it, to maneuver into position on either side of it. Then Damius Rawlings hopped inside the jeep and they were driving onto the boat. Other cars came on. And last, people walking hurried to the few blue molded plastic seats situated in a section in front of the cars. Heavy chains secured the cars for the trip.

Junius and his father got out of the jeep, joining

other passengers who stood along the deck rail. The seat section was behind them centered on deck. There was a canvas awning stretched above the seats.

The ferry horn sounded, and they were underway. Junius grinned; so did Damius Rawlings. They stood at the rail with wind in their faces. Cooler now, as they went out of the port to sea. Junius looked back once. They left a wide, foamy wake behind them. The big island was fast retreating. In no time, mountains faded into mist.

"Never in my life!" Junius murmured.

He saw all the sights, all the smaller islands and atolls that Grandfather must have seen on his way to the Snake. They were like monstrous sea creatures darkly rising out of the water as the ferry went by them. The sun brightened their shining surfaces of verdant hills and folds and rock outcroppings.

Great sheets of spray were lifted by the wind as the boat swayed through the waves. It hit the decks and ran down the awning. Water dribbled onto people sitting beneath. People laughed, moved over a little. The spray was warm; nobody minded getting wet.

Junius learned what sea swells were. His father told him that was what it was called when the ocean gathered in great heaves. The heaves of sea bulged and expanded. Swells were simply waves that rolled but did not break.

The ferry rode the sea, swooping up the swells and crashing down them. It feels much like a roller coaster,

dontcha know, Junius thought, and then: I am following the way of Grandfather Jackabo home. He tried
to see everything as Grandfather would have. All at
once he thought of Sarrietta.

Wish you were here, girl, he thought. Cannot explain to you how the sea looks, how the air feels. How
much I care for you! Do you still care for me? Does
Plas bother you now? Oh, I am jealous just thinkin'
about it! So don't think about it.

"Junius, look," his father said, pointing.

Fish exploded out of the water as the boat passed.
They seemed to have wings. Their pectoral fins were
indeed winglike.

"Flying fish, Junius," his father said.

"Ha! Look!" Junius exclaimed, as one after another,
fish leaped and sailed for quite a distance before falling
back into the sea again. Grandfahtha seen them and
now Junius son has seen them, he thought.

The ferry was deep at sea. Atolls they had passed
were in the misty distance behind. Junius watched the
water long after the flying fish had disappeared. He
daydreamed pirates and great sailing ships. He fought
with a sword and dagger to save the dark-eyed damsel,
Sarrietta, and heard only the throb of the ferry engines.

All at once someone across deck at the starboard rail
began shouting, "DAW-FAH! DAW-FAH!"

"Junius, come!" his father urged, pulling him by the
arm. Then he and his father and everybody else who
had been leaning on the port rail rushed to starboard.

"Daw-fah!"

"Fahtha, what is it?" Junius asked.

"Watch," said his father.

The six-foot swells carrying the ferry up and over smoothly were dark blue, almost black, and shining full. The sun beat down. "Daw-fah!" people cried out, pointing down at the sea. There was dark, swift movement in a shining inkwell of ocean. Junius spied something there. In a moment he saw two creatures.

"Dolphins," his father said.

"No, really, it can't be!" Junius exclaimed. But it was certainly dolphins. Their sleek skins were almost the same dark as the ocean. Junius was able to separate them from sea swells by their grayer color. Without warning they leaped in their characteristic, swift curve. It was a wonderful sight. People hollered out each time the dolphins leaped. He shouted, too. All the passengers were of one voice, urging the dolphins on. Junius knew he must have joined some renowned club, and one had to travel by ferry to join. He felt close to the people, many of whom had speech patterns like his and Grandfather Jackabo's.

I am an island mahn for true, Junius thought, and Grandfahtha, too. Fahtha don't want to be one, but I think that he is one, way deep inside himself somewhere.

The dolphins stayed with the ferry, disappearing under the sea and then appearing again, for an hour or more.

"Seeing that brings back memories," said his father, watching the dolphins cavort.

"Does it? When you lived in the islands?" Junius asked. He leaned close to his father, looking up at him.

Damius nodded. "When your grandfather was a younger man and we would go in the open current, open sea between islands. We had a good, sturdy boat— funny, I haven't thought about it in years. And we would catch grouper and other large fish. I remember I would feel that we were far away from home. But I wasn't scared of anything out there. I felt safe and at peace."

"That's nice," Junius said. I would surely like to go in a boat with you, he thought. But he felt shy about saying it. He wondered if his father would like going fishing with him.

Junius sighed, staring at the sea. He felt light-headed a bit, but not seasick. The time went by swiftly, and it seemed like no time at all before Snake Island came into view. The dolphins had apparently gone for good. Junius waited, studying the sea swells, but they did not return. They took a piece of Junius' heart with them. He thought a farewell to them: Go along, you son and daughter of the sea. Hope to see you on the way back home!

Snake Island. His father, pointing. Telling Junius what it was he just noticed looming darkly off to the left on the horizon. Snake Island. It rose out of the sea like a mirage. The ferryboat drew closer. Soon the island appeared clearly; it looked serene. There were white clouds above the land, making shade. Sunlight went on and off on green-and-brown hills of Snake Island. Over far.

The sea was turquoise now, and clear. The Snake was coiled in upon itself. Its beaches winked at Junius, like yellow moon eyes.

"That one over there is called Tamarind," his father said, pointing to a beach. "Named after the tamarind trees that have yellow flowers streaked red and big, brown pods. . . ." His voice trailed off.

"Fahtha, can we go there sometime?" Junius asked.

"We'll visit beaches you've never dreamed," said his father. "Everything looks just the same."

Why did you wait so long? Junius wanted to ask him. But something told him his father would have to search awhile for the answer to that.

Lawrence, Snake Island, was not at all what Junius had expected. The streets were narrow, hilly, and the town was stifling hot. There were no sea breezes flowing through the twisting streets. Everything baked dustily under a burning sun.

People from the boat streamed by the jeep. Cars and people in separate lines climbed steeply from the dock. There were food shops, a boat equipment and diving shop. Junius noticed a small hotel facing the sea, which was at a distance below now, and a Seaside Restaurant. There was a gas station and a small park with a tiny band platform. It overlooked the shoreline.

Junius looked back. He could see the dock again, and boys diving off it into the water. Now that the ferry had arrived, young people had taken over the dock to sit and to chat. Everything was confusion, crowds, and heat. Somehow, it all seemed less than Junius had expected. All the shops were smaller, less prosperous than he would have wished. At once he sensed that fresh water was precious here. For people walking or riding carried at least one container of water with them. He noticed differences from the big island. There was a tiny ice-cream shop, just a window in a wall, really, and it served one flavor of ice cream, vanilla, with one flavor topping, which was chocolate syrup.

Funny what you see and notice, he thought. The heat! Where did the breeze go? He was soaking with perspiration.

"Tired?" asked his father. He looked anxiously at their surroundings.

"I think I must be," Junius answered. "I think I would like somethin' to drink."

"The heat gets to you, until you get used to it. It's been a long time since I've felt heat like this," his father said. "We'll get something to drink in a minute."

They drove to a small neighborhood grocery. Junius stayed in the jeep, looking at everything. There was a church down the street on the other side, at the corner. It had a beautiful tree with flaming red flowers on the tiny plot of land in front of it.

His father called him to help with the grocery sacks. They placed the sacks in the back of the jeep. Damius had bought a sleeping bag. "For you," he told Junius. "You're the youngest. And according to Father's letters, there are two bedrooms and only two beds."

He bought them each a cold can of soda pop. Junius drank and drank. In a minute the can had grown lukewarm in his hand, the heat of the day was that strong.

They were on their way again through the town. Little houses, all colors, so close to the cobblestoned street. Junius felt he might just reach out and touch the doorknobs. Then they were driving out of town, bumping along the rutted, rain-muddied coast road. The road wound along a steep hillside above an immense bay. The hillside went up and up, to the right of the road. The bay was to their left. The deep bay, Grandfather had called it. Junius recognized it at once. They had come in to dock on the other side of the island. The Snake wound itself around, hiding the bay from view. It was an absolutely grand bay, grand island!

Junius looked on at sailboats that lazily sailed the bay channel out to sea, or came in from somewhere. He saw tiny houses built on barrels right out from the shore, no land under them at all. But each house had a dock with at least one boat tied to it. The windows of the houses were open, doors open to the breeze off the bay. Young people lay out on wooden decks in just swimming trunks. In hammocks. Were they vacationers or islanders? It was impossible to tell. But this was an easy outdoor way of life. An altogether different way of living from what Junius had ever known. Island sun, island clouds, island sea. Island life. No snow or cold anywhere. To think that all this had been going on for an eternity without him! He glanced over at his father and wondered again how it was possible he had put so much distance between himself and his land.

Grandfahtha Jackabo does know, Junius thought. He does know what paradise is, and where it tis.

The hillside above the road grew steeper. There was a cliff up there, and on top of the cliff was a house that commanded a view of the whole bay. There was another road off the coast road leading up to the house. They went around the bulge of the hillside and they could see across a portion of the bay.

"Pelican Cove," his father murmured.

Pelican Cove. Junius hadn't imagined it would be so large. And sweeping out from it, out beyond the cove, was the bay, surrounded by high hills and cliffs, as far as he could see from left to right. To one side of the cove was a dock with a boat tied to it.

"See the dory!" Junius said.

"And look up there," his father told him.

Your eyes just sweep straight up from the dock, Junius thought. Up from the hillside. I can't see the path up but it tis there. Oh, I know it tis.

There was a small building over to the left on the hillside. Above that, another low building. The bedrooms of Grandfahtha and Burtie! But at the top of the hill was the sight. The beauty of an old mansion could not be equaled. There it sat in its ruined splendor. Full in the light it was; the sunlight made it look almost new. The plantation house of Burtie Rawlings. The Rawlings lands. Their same name, too.

"Fahtha, let's go!"

The coast road wound around the cove. Soon they were in a low place where mangroves grew right to the side of the road, where Junius could feel the cool ocean breeze and could hear the water lapping at tree roots when his father stopped the car a moment.

"See? The road goes to the top of the hill," his father said. "But we'll turn here." They turned at the lane that passed below the Rawlings hillside. Damius Rawlings stopped the jeep. He and Junius were getting out when they saw—at first they weren't sure what they saw.

# Fifteen

A sweet-looking, decidedly dirty, baldheaded, and very bowlegged old mahn appeared from the high weeds along the path in front of Junius and his father. He was so darkened from the sun that he looked as if he had been scorched by a fire. His cloak was filthy. Mimis swarmed around his ears. His legs trembled as he swayed before them, leaning on his staff. His face broke into pieces; tears welled up in his eyes and spilled down his face. His mouth sagged; there were no teeth in his mouth. His hands were clasped tightly in prayer.

Grandfahtha. It was a startling moment, but it dawned right away on Junius, and on Damius, that this filthy old man was Grandfather Jackabo. Junius' own grandfather, come to this!

He put his teeth down somewhere and forgot where, Junius was thinking. A sharp cry of anguish escaped him.

Grandfather Jackabo had no trousers or walking shorts on, just his underwear. His skinny legs were slashed and crossed with scrapes and bruises. His ankles were gray-black with dust and muddy hillside dirt. Most likely, he had meant to wash his trousers. But clothes washing would take so much of his energy, Junius decided. Probably Grandfather had left his trousers somewhere and he didn't remember where. All Junius could think of was that he had abandoned his grandfather, who was perhaps ill and maybe starving. Looking half crazed from loneliness.

Damius Rawlings' pulse beat like a drum in his neck. He saw an anguished old man, deprived of simple decency. He had a mental image, suddenly, of his father, an old, revered one in the rain forest of his homeland. But then the old one was taken, separated from his tribe by the slave ships. His father, the African lost forever on a foreign shore.

What have I done to him? Damius thought. He went to his father and folded him close. "Father! Hello! All right now. It's all right!" Damius soothed. "We're here; we've brought food, too. We'll take care of you, don't worry."

Damius would have asked a hundred questions, but now was not the time or place.

"My boy!" exclaimed Grandfather Jackabo. His voice trembled.

"Oh, Father! Have you actually been all alone way out here?" Damius asked.

"I . . . I been alone since My Old Enemy taken away by them bloodthirsty pirates," Grandfather Jackabo moaned. "I don't know how long that be. Ha! I thought you never be coming, son. I thought you done be forgettin' about me; and the bloody pirates come back and does take me away one day, too."

"How could we ever forget about you?" Damius said, holding old Jackabo by the arms, then reaching to touch his face.

Grandfather grinned and pulled back from his son. He looked over at Junius, who waited to be recognized in a way that was proper. Junius came forward then and entered the circle of his father's and grandfather's love.

Grandfather Jackabo laughed and patted him, as though Junius and he had never been apart. He grinned and pointed at the jeep. "Son!" Grandfather grinned at Damius. "Take us for a ride! Take Junius son and me to the top of Rawlings hill. Then Junius son see it all!"

Damius Rawlings sighed, hesitating. He wanted to get the food he had bought on impulse in town out of the heat. He wanted to get his father cleaned up and taken care of.

"Fahtha, please do what he wants," Junius murmured. Grandfather had hold of his arm and was pulling him to the jeep. He cackled happily. Junius smiled. "Grandfahtha, I'm so happy to see you. I am one happy island mahn this day!"

"Hee, hee!" laughed Grandfather Jackabo. "Me too, me too!"

They got into the jeep and Damius took them up. It was a hard, rutty ride nearly straight up. But it didn't take long. They turned onto the old coach road and pulled up at the house.

The silence at the summit was very new to Junius. The grand, abandoned house was history right before him. He knew he loved the Rawlings lands, the house. But Grandfather Jackabo pulled him away from the house and out across the coach road close to the downslope of the hill's far side.

"Dah!" Grandfather said.

And so it was. There, the astounding horseshoe of land and sea, with the headland of Medusa Point to the left. The sweep of blues and browns and yellows, of birds and flowers. Wind that was almost cool, but never quite, the rest was silence in Junius' ears. The awesome view stirred him deeply. He breathed it in with his eyes, never to forget.

Damius Rawlings spoke quietly to Junius, remembering the names of Medusa Point and Medusa Beach. Telling that this was the headland of the island, that perhaps the best swimming reef was out there at Medusa Beach. That they would go there one day soon.

"These Rawlings lands are where our ancestors lived and slaved and died," his father said.

He doesn't want to have to explain about it, I can tell, Junius thought, but I'm grateful that he will.

"We don't know what their original names were or where they came from, how they suffered to get here," Damius said. "But that's another story for another time."

"Tis nothing," Grandfather Jackabo spoke, all at once. "It tis everything! Slaves, my people. I show you where the slave lads sat. You can still see the feet of them in the cement."

"Grandfahtha, I want to see that," Junius said.

"Now, we must go down," said Damius. He would have avoided all this if he could have. He would have forever disallowed the past. Would he?

Junius helped Grandfather. Grandfather Jackabo clung to him, staring up at him, drinking him in.

"My boat does good!" Grandfather told him as they headed back across the road. Damius had started the jeep. Its sputter reminded Grandfather about the dory. "It fine, motor fine. But since My Old Enemy taken by the buccaneers, I can't dock it right by myself, dontcha see?"

"Grandfahtha, it be all right," said Junius, softly. He had said little since seeing Grandfather. He held old Jackabo close.

Grandfahtha has no weight to him, Junius thought. He is most like a spirit, floating. He felt a lump in his throat. "Grandfahtha, get in," he said, gently. "We must put everything away."

They went back down in the jeep. And it wasn't until they were at the foot of the hill looking up at the Rawlings house high above that Grandfather remembered where the refrigerator was. He cackled and explained.

Junius and his father smiled tiredly. Something about the sad situation struck Junius as funny. He giggled. Before he knew it, his father was chuckling. Soon they were all laughing. They tired themselves out laughing. But it relieved the tension. And then Junius saw Grandfather's chair situated on the path, halfway up the hillside. It seemed to be at rest there, as though gazing at the sea—such a curious sight it was.

"Look! Look!" Junius exclaimed, pointing. The chair was formal, empty in the tall grass, a vacated throne left by a wandering king.

They laughed until it hurt.

"Nothing to do but go back up the hill," Damius said when they had calmed down. The three of them climbed in the jeep again and drove to the top of the hill. For the second time Junius saw that grand sweep of open sky and sea. All was not lost. They found the refrigerator, humming in the shadows of its coolish room. And they put the food away.

Grandfahtha. Hard to believe this be the same day as this mornin' on the ferry, Junius thought. He and Grandfather were now at the long table in the kitchen on the Rawlings hillside. Junius had fitted his feet over the smaller cement footprints of slave lads and felt protective of what little was left of them there in the room. He told Grandfather about the ferry.

"So much has happened," Junius said. Grandfather Jackabo sat at the head of the table. Junius sat to one side on his right.

Grandfather smiled happily at him. He had shed his tunic cloak so they could wash it. He now wore a T-shirt. Junius had found his teeth for him. He looked less thin with his teeth in. The two of them were drinking ice-cold lemonade and eating fried bologna sandwiches. Junius had made the lemonade and the sandwiches for their late lunch. It was about one-thirty in the afternoon now. He had finally quenched his thirst with the lemonade, drinking glass after glass of it. His job now was to keep Grandfather company while his father took care of things on the hillside. Everything they drank tasted of bleach, which was what Burtie had used to purify the water, Grandfather said. And everything was dirty. Dust and sand from the wind, mostly. Mud from the rains, from the hillside, tracked in all over. The bedrooms hadn't been cleaned for a long time. His father took buckets of water and cleansers, cleaning floors, tabletops, counters in the kitchen and bathroom.

Junius had finished up the kitchen counters and cleaned out some of the cupboards. Throwing away packaged food that was so old, it had become mealy. Ants were everywhere anything spilled. He'd have to be careful the plastic garbage bags were closed tightly, his father warned. Their garbage would have to be taken into town to the public barrels on the town dock.

But not for a couple of days. Now his father was off at the forecourt, working on the bedrooms, scrubbing and spraying the floors and corners against insects. Of course, lizards got in everywhere, his father had told him. But lizards were harmless.

Junius watched one now, on the wall. It was a very strange, small, dry-looking creature. It had the ability to inflate its throat like a balloon. He wondered about it. Lizards always seemed to be watching.

He loved everything about the Rawlings lands. For one thing, they had the same name as he and that made him feel closer to them, somehow. He loved the kitchen off on the hillside by itself. Loved running up the steep hill through the spreading gandules—now he knew what they were; Grandfather had showed him, singing his gandules song. Up the steep hill to the silent manor house and creeping through ghostly hallways to get to the refrigerator. He had to remember to keep in mind all the items they might need from the refrigerator each time they ate. Mayonnaise and mustard, the bread, the bologna. Ice and icewater, lemons for the lemonade. Junius had to make two extra trips to the top of the hill because he hadn't taken the time to memorize what he needed. Oatmeal cookies for a snack.

"I don't mind climbing the hillside," he told Grandfather Jackabo.

"Young legs!" Grandfather announced, through his chewing.

"Yes! I have strong legs, dontcha see?" Junius said,

and stuck one long, young, strong leg out for Grandfather to see.

He had changed his shorts. He wore no shirt, it was that hot. The less clothes, the better, he was quick to learn.

"When the shadows come, you must put a shirt on," Grandfather said. He meant when the sun left the hillside. "And if you perspire in the sun, you must put a shirt on. The mimis always come." It was true, they did come.

The kitchen had been cleaned and seemed to be free now of larger insects. But mimis appeared out of nowhere to circle the crumbs on Junius' plate and the bologna sandwich in his hand. His bare legs and chest.

By the time the sun hung poised high above the west hills, Junius knew the whole story of Burtie Rawlings' disappearance exactly as Grandfather told it. Grandfather had gone through the story as they sat in the kitchen. Then he said he must go to take a nap. "I am happy you will share my room, Junius son," he said in parting.

"I am happy too, Grandfahtha," Junius said. He was to sleep in Grandfather's forecourt room in the sleeping bag, while his father took Burtie Rawlings' room. Grandfather looked relieved and pleased about the arrangement.

Junius took what was perishable back to the refrigerator. Then he and Damius checked the cistern. It was nearly half full of rainwater. Next, they washed the clothes they had traveled to the big island in, and also Grandfather's trousers and cloak and a few bath towels and dish towels they'd found lying about. They heated water on the kitchen stove and poured it into a metal tub that Grandfather said old Burtie had used for clothes washing. Once the clothes were washed and rinsed, they began hanging them on the line by the tool shed. Junius and his father had a chance to talk together, alone.

"Grandfahtha forgets some things. And he was surely not eatin' right, not eatin' enough," Junius said. "But we will take care of that now. I think he'll be fine in a few days, Fahtha."

"Yes, I think you're right," his father said.

"He says that men, pirates, came and took Burtie Rawlings away," Junius said.

"That's what he wrote in his last letter, too," his father said. "But it worries me. His mind, the talk about pirates."

"He seems so certain that that is what happened. Maybe it tis true," said Junius. "Maybe men did take Burtie away. Not pirates, that must be just Grand-fahtha's fear. But men, after somethin'?"

"Maybe. But what would men want with old Burtie Rawlings living out his days here on this run-down estate?" said his father.

"I've been thinkin' about that, Fahtha," Junius said.

"Grandfahtha talk about that house over there. That Koster or Kostera house?"

"Yes? I remember that in the letter."

"Well, Grandfahtha tell it, too, saying that Burtie was always watchin' that house with his binoculars. And he didn't want Grandfahtha to know he was watchin', that's what Grandfahtha tell me. And so Burtie watched when he thought Grandfahtha was away on the boat or sittin' down there on the dock. Only Grandfahtha found out he was watchin'. Do you think there be some connection to that house and the pirates? Grandfahtha never say that, but I was wonderin' that."

Damius shook his head. "I found no binoculars anywhere around, Junius. If there are no binoculars, how could Burtie have been watching that house?"

"None? No binoculars?" said Junius.

"None anywhere. I looked in the kitchen, this shed. I searched the house up there. I look in Burtie's room and Grandfather's. There are no binoculars."

"I don't know, then," Junius said. "It all began makin' sense to me. But if there are no binoculars. . . . But still," Junius went on, "Grandfahtha never changes the story of the pirates."

"Yes, that's true," his father said. "That *is* interesting." He sighed. Finished with hanging the clothes, he stood there, looking off far out toward the deep bay.

"Maybe we'll go into town tomorrow," Mr. Rawlings said. "Pay a visit to the constable there. There is the one single fact that we are sure of," he said.

"And that is?" Junius said.

"That Burtie Rawlings is not here. That Burtie Rawlings has disappeared from the Rawlings Estate without a trace. Someone should be told that."

"I thought we would go swimmin' tomorrow," Junius said, and was at once sorry he had said that. The seriousness of the situation suddenly hit him. How could he think of swimming when a mahn was missing?

"Tomorrow is a long day, like today," his father said. "We'll see about swimming. First things first. We can take the boat into town, Junius."

"All the way in the dory!" Junius said. He grinned. "Oh, I want to go down to that dock today! I want to stand on it, dontcha know. I want to see that boat!"

# Sixteen

It was the hour after their leisurely late lunch, after Junius had talked with his father and Grandfather had had his nap. Junius found himself laughing all the time now at almost anything. Standing on the hillside, his arm around Grandfather Jackabo, he grinned up at the sky, at the very hot, tropic day. He breathed deeply of the Snake, saw the starlike frangipani, Grandfather called it, on the far shore, and the wild palms, and he was content beyond words.

He and Grandfather Jackabo went down the hillside. Grandfather held on to his arm. The two of them were so close, and had been so all afternoon, just enjoying one another. Old Jackabo was so happy. He looked into Junius' face as if he could not get enough of seeing the resemblance there to his own boy, Damius, and to himself.

Junius, too, drank in the sight of his grandfather's tiny self. Grandfather Jackabo's eyes grew more alert.

Junius knew, beyond his years, how cruel was heartache, how fragile was life.

They went carefully down, picking their way. Junius led, going down sideways and holding tightly to Grandfather's free hand. In the other hand Grandfather had his staff, which was still a great help to him. They made their way down in the high heat of the afternoon. But neither of them felt it very much, nor noticed the annoying mimis. They were busy talking. Grandfather talked about the too-tall guinea grass and how Damius and Junius would need to cut it.

"You will use the machetes, sharp blades. My Old Enemy keep them in the toolshed, dontcha know."

"Not to worry, Grandfahtha, Fahtha and I will take care of it," Junius told him.

"I'll not worry, Junius son, now that you have come to live with me."

At the foot of the hill was a well-worn path. To the left of the path, off a ways, were twisted and tangled mangroves growing out of the water, making shade all along the bank.

"There are land crabs in there, where it tis wet," said Grandfather, pausing a moment. "Crabs are good to eat, if you digging them out."

"It looks secret in there, and dark," Junius said, eyeing the hushed mangroves.

"Stinging eels in there—stay away, Junius son."

Junius looked, and listened to the water lapping at

the mangroves. All was exciting, and mysterious, too. They walked along the path down a steep bank to the dock. The dock was somewhat rickety, but it would not fall in on itself this day. The wood planks were weathered gray. There were metal posts along the sides to hold on to. The waters of Pelican Cove flowed right under the dock, and the dock extended out from the land. There was the dory floating on the water, its mooring lines tied up to a dock post.

"See the current?" Grandfather said. "The current swings the boat always that way.

"Look there"—Grandfather pointed—"in the shallowest water, dontcha see? A starfish, livin' right there, too. And two cucumbers."

Junius spotted the beautiful orange starfish on the bottom. The water was astonishingly clear and the starfish was really there.

"It tis alive, you say? It lies so still," he whispered.

"Oh, it does be very alive," said Grandfather. "You will not see starfish move. But every day, it will move from where it was the evening before."

"It must move slowly, then," Junius said.

"Oh, very slowly, in time with the moon, perhaps. The moon move very slowly in some way, although it travel fast, too," said Grandfather.

"Yes," Junius whispered. "Where are the cucumbers?" he asked. "Why did you throw them away—don't you like to eat them?"

Grandfather Jackabo laughed, shaking his head. "Not cucumbers from a garden! Hee, hee! But sea cucumbers!"

"I've never heard of them," Junius said.

Grandfather pointed to a place in the water very near the shore and almost under the dock. There were two shapes, one orange and one pale, almost white. They were plump and slimy-looking, shaped like cucumbers. They lay very still, side by side.

"Alive?" Junius asked.

"Oh, very alive," said Grandfather, "but very sluggish."

"How awfully strange life can be!" said Junius.

Grandfather said nothing. He had turned around toward the dory. "See how low the boat sits," he said. "It tis very hard for an old mahn to get in and out of a dory by himself. Dock is up too high. An old mahn do have too far to stumble and fall. And too high to climb and scrape his arms."

"I see," said Junius. He studied the situation. "But now a mahn who is not so really old has his grandson to help him, even though the poor grandson is too afraid to jump down there so far on the water."

"Hee, hee!" giggled Grandfather. "Surely the mahns may help each other."

Junius sat on the dock, at Grandfather's direction. The dock was quite warm from the sun. He pulled on the mooring line from the boat, pulling the dory nearly to the dock. When he had it as close as it would come to the side, Junius stepped down on a crosspiece. The dory rocked and he sat down hard on the seat. Grandfather laughed. Then, very carefully, Junius helped Grandfather down. They were staggering and laughing by the time Grandfather stepped up on the prow.

"Such poor, little sea legs!" Grandfather teased Junius. "There is a rhythm to it, dontcha see?" he said. Once in the boat, he was as agile as a cat. He stood on the swaying prow with hardly any effort. Junius had to sit down and hold on. A boat was quite a new experience for him.

"Oh, I like this very much!" he told Grandfather, and looked around expectantly.

"It tis too late in the day for me to start up the motor, son," Grandfather Jackabo explained. "I am much too old to have strength that lasts all day. When I get in the boat by myself, I save my strength for it. I did not do that today."

"No matter, Grandfahtha," Junius said. He enjoyed just sitting, feeling the boat bob slowly up and down under him. It made him slightly dizzy at first, but soon that went away.

Grandfather took out fishing lines from under the prow. There was not any bait, but they could try. He thought of something else and crawled through the little doors and halfway into the space under the prow.

"What tis it, Grandfahtha?" Junius said.

Jackabo crawled out and pulled himself with some amount of discomfort onto the seat. Just then Damius came down from the hillside to join them.

"Hello!" Junius called to him.

"Hunh?" Grandfather said, turning. He saw his son. "Oh, Damius son, it tis you."

"Yes, Father. I see the two of you are having a ride." He was relieved to find that Junius still kept his father company.

"Come join us!" Junius said. His father stood there on the dock in the shade. He had finished cleaning up the place and had showered, Junius supposed. Damius had on jeans and a short-sleeved shirt. That was usually about as casual as his father ever got. Tall and very lean, he now looked more like an island mahn, truly, Junius thought.

"Have you eaten? You want me to make you a sandwich?" Junius asked him.

"I had lemonade. It's too hot for me to eat yet," his father answered.

"Damius, I cannot find the gun," Grandfather said, abruptly. "I look here in the boat where I put it. I wrap it in wax paper against the salt air, and it tis not here. It tis gone and I cannot remember where it walk away! Huh."

Damius Rawlings stood very still. Slowly it came to him about the gun, from one of his father's letters. He'd forgotten about it. Then he moved and quickly stepped down into the dory. He bent over to look in the space below the prow. The gun was not there. He thought that the gun had gone the way of the binoculars. There was no trusting his father's memory anymore. If the lost items were anywhere around, perhaps they would turn up again.

"Maybe I leave it in My Old Enemy's drawer beside his bed. Maybe I put it back where I got it."

Very slowly, Damius turned to look at his father. "What?" he said.

"Maybe I put it back there in the drawer," Grandfather repeated.

Junius looked from his father to Grandfather Jackabo and back. His father's face took on a puzzled expression. Damius sat down on the prow. He stared at his feet, as the boat moved lazily in a short arch on gentle swells. All was still. Water lapped against the dock, that was all.

Grandfather was quiet. He had begun fishing with just a line and a hook. Junius also had a line, and he let his line dangle in the water, but he did not expect to hook anything. He didn't. Neither did Grandfather. His father remained strangely silent, just sitting. In a half hour, the three of them returned to the stifling hillside. Junius helped Grandfather. His father climbed in front of them, with his hands deep in his pockets and his head down.

It had been a wonderful day, Junius was thinking. From the ferryboat ride clear to now.

By the time he and Grandfather were most of the way up, his father was at the very top of the hill disappearing around the portico of the great house.

And while Junius was getting Grandfather and himself lemonade in the kitchen, his father came back from the hilltop with supplies for supper gathered together in a carton.

At evening Damius made a fine supper of yellow rice and chicken, and gandules and onions and tomatoes, all in one pot. Grandfather Jackabo had supplied the gandules. It had been Junius's job to set the table and make a lettuce salad and help his father clean up afterward. His father had cooked the chicken and rice.

"Why it taste soooo good?" Junius wanted to know, repeatedly helping himself from the pot.

"It tis being so close to the sea," Grandfather said. "It tis this place under the sun. Gives a mahn sense to enjoy what tis given him."

"That must be it," Junius said. "It sure give me my appetite back, too!"

The sky was streaked with blues and purples, reds and oranges of a perfect setting sun as they ate. They were a respectful audience, staring out through the screens. The dying sun, the sky, the hills and bay, had performed for them. And the curtain of night gradually came down. Later, there rose a fine, white moon.

The moon rose to one side of the great house at the hilltop. Junius went outside to look at the tropic moon. Until his being out there with yellow spiders about to pounce on him made Grandfather nervous. Junius had done the dishes and put them away while his father returned leftovers to the refrigerator. His father said that climbing to and from the hilltop would be his daily exercise. Then Junius and Grandfather hurried to the forecourt through the darkness into the safety of their rooms.

Damius had found pieces of wood planking neatly stacked in the toolshed. Burtie Rawlings most likely kept the odds and ends for minor repairs about the Rawlings property. In no time Damius had put together a platform for Junius' sleeping bag. And Junius and Grandfather Jackabo now rested comfortably in Grandfather's room. For Grandfather would not hear of Junius spreading the sleeping bag on the bare floor and sleeping that way.

"No, no, no!" he had hollered in warning. "There are waterbugs here, come creeping, oh, awful! And scorpions. And sometimes even Fahtha Tarantula come. Never sleep on the floor, Junius son. No, no no! At all times, be watching where you lie and where the feet does go."

Junius was very interested in seeing a tarantula and a scorpion, and he told Grandfather Jackabo, "Such are creatures of the islands, just like me and you!" He was teasing Grandfather a bit, too.

Grandfather slapped the side of his head in shock. "You going to claim them?" he said to Junius. "You going to call them cousin when they drop on you from the ceiling? They live in nests! Now, Nulio, he my giant turtle come along under my boat—"

"Really?" Junius said. "A giant turtle, and he comin' to you—Nulio? You talk about Nulio in one of your letters, I recall."

Grandfather didn't remember that. But he remembered Nulio then; also, his dream of Nulio. "He climb in the dory to rest, and we talk awhile," Grandfather said.

Junius laughed. He thought Grandfather Jackabo must be joking. But Grandfather did not smile; and he forgot about Nulio.

Both Junius and Grandfather felt refreshed and content, settling down for the night. They had had showers in the working bathroom, rather than beside the cistern. The shower had a compact electric mechanism that fitted to the water pipe of the shower head. When the faucet was turned on, the pressure of water through the mechanism heated the water coming out of the shower head. A fine invention to counter the cool-water cistern system of the Caribbean islands.

Junius was on his platform, a few feet over from Grandfather's bed. The platform was almost twelve inches above the floor. It was hard, yes, but not uncomfortable. He was lying atop the sleeping bag, wearing just shorts and a T-shirt to sleep in. The night was very warm. Grandfather was sitting on his bed wearing new seersucker pajamas that Damius had brought him from home. His feet did not touch the floor. He eagerly watched his grandson. He looked somewhat tired, but happy and quite clean.

Damius came in to say good night. He stood by the door. Junius smiled at him. Damius was looking at Grandfather Jackabo. He sighed once, deeply, and then he said, "Father, have you been in Burtie's room lately?"

"Huh?" Grandfather said.

"I said, when was the last time you visited Burtie Rawlings' room?"

"You mean, where you sleeping now?" Grandfather said.

"Yes," said Damius.

Grandfather thought a moment and Junius said, "Why? Why do you want to know, Fahtha?"

His father looked at him sharply but did not answer. He waited for Grandfather.

"Been a while," Grandfather finally said.

Damius was quiet a moment. "Do you mind coming into Burtie's room now?" Damius asked.

Grandfather looked at him. He found his flip-flop slippers, put them on, still looking at Damius. "You find the gun, then?" he said, in the softest voice.

Damius shook his head, came over, and helped his father up. Junius didn't ask if he could come. He simply followed, bewildered by the way his father was acting. He had seen Burtie Rawlings' room earlier today. He remembered that he and his father had put his father's things there. It hadn't made any impression on him, particuarly. And then Junius had taken his own things to Grandfather's room, where Grandfather had hurried around making space for him.

Grandfather Jackabo stood there in Burtie's room with his mouth opened. He looked all around. He touched the bed, patted it, and nodded, as if to say, "Truly, here does be My Old Enemy's bed."

He stretched out his hand to touch the end table where Burtie had kept his gun. He patted thin air, for the end table was not there. As if dazed, Grandfather shuffled over to the cabinet just behind the bed, where Burtie kept some papers. He went to touch it, but there was nothing there to touch. And then he slowly made his way to the empty space where the trestle table had been.

"Ahhhhh," said Grandfather. He shook his head. He put his hand to his forehead. "His silver urn does be gone one day," he said. "And that pretty cloth does be gone, too. But that mahogany table be there all the time. It does! Mahogany, very old, made from Snake Island mahogany, dontcha know. Plenty mahogany trees long ago. Fine mahogany!"

"Father, you say there was a silver urn that disappeared first?" Damius asked.

Grandfather nodded. "And a silken throw always to cover the table. The silver urn sit on that silken cloth all the time. But they both gone, and he be taken by pirates."

Grandfather walked toward the screen door. He looked down to one side of the door, then over at Damius. "Used to be a stool right here. I sit on it every time. It quite comfortable, too. I drop the gandules—

did I? But maybe I just be dreamin' up furniture and gandules. Did we eat gandules for supper?"

Damius nodded. "You had gandules for supper and you have not been dreaming, not this time, Father. I cleaned up a pile of rotted pods right by the door."

Grandfather ran his hand over his eyes. "I . . ." he began, but did not finish.

"There was furniture every place you said—you can see the impressions," said Damius.

Junius began to understand. Besides the bed, there had been other furniture in the room. And that furniture was now missing. It was what had disturbed his father down at the dock. Grandfather had mentioned putting a gun back in a drawer, but his father knew there was no drawer.

Nothin' is where it should be, Junius thought. No Burtie and no Burtie's belongings. If that table was there after Burtie was taken, then . . .

He stared at his father with growing understanding and apprehension, too. He caught his father's warning look and didn't say anything.

Something is surely goin' on . It tis all true! Pirates did come here. And somebody been right here again!

# Seventeen

Damius Rawlings made a soft, high whistling to rouse Junius without waking Grandfather Jackabo. Up later than usual the night before, Grandfather Jackabo still slept soundly.

The noise was irritating. It broke through Junius' sleep. He woke up in a sweat, feeling hot and uncomfortable. His father was outside at the screen door. Junius got up and walked silently to the door. "What time it tis?" he whispered.

"Nine thirty," his father spoke softly back. "We need to get into town by eleven. The whole town closes at about noon and opens again at three. Get your clothes—let's go."

Junius grabbed clean jeans and a cotton shirt. He put on tennis shoes without socks and hurried to the bathroom to wash and dress. When he came out, he heard his father down the hill in the kitchen, and he went down.

"Fahtha," he said, coming in, "shouldn't I wake Grandfahtha, ask him if he would not care to go with us into town?"

"We're going to try using the boat," said his father. "And I think we'll go without Grandfather. We'll let him rest. You could leave him a note so he'll know."

Junius wrote a note on tablet paper and took it back to the forecourt room. He left it positioned on his sleeping bag, where Grandfather would be sure to see it. When he turned to leave, Grandfather was smiling at him.

"Son, Junius," he said. "I thought at first I does dream you here and you no island mahn atall."

"Grandfahtha, I'm here. I am really here! And it's one of the beautiful days you wrote me about. All sun and heat and everything. Listen. Fahtha and I go into town. He thought we let you rest some today."

"Good idea, I think," said Grandfather. "It take me too long, half a day, to get me fit enough and breakfast and rest again and down the hill, and rest again. Oh, it take me forever almost. You go ahead. I be here when you return."

"Do you want me to make your breakfast?" asked Junius. "Some pancakes, maybe. Some French toast. I know how to make that very fast."

Grandfather thought about French toast. "With syrup and a little nutmeg?"

"We have it all in the kitchen now," Junius told him.

"Maybe tomorrow," Grandfather said, and closed

his eyes. "I feel as if I could lie here the whole day. Knowing you and Damius be here taking care of everything."

"I'm goin', Grandfahtha," Junius said to him, patting his arm. "We are taking the dory, dontcha see, if it be all right."

Grandfather smiled and nodded but didn't open his eyes.

"Do you think I will see Nulio, the turtle, on our way?" Junius asked.

Now Grandfather opened his eyes. "Nulio go the other way," he said. "He go in the Shallows to find lots of rocks and he look like rocks, too. And you go in the deep bay. He know better than be bait for somebody come along with a spear gun. It does be illegal to spear the great turtles. But there are people who try to get away with what they can."

"When will I get to see the Shallows?"

"Maybe when you come back or maybe tomorrow, we go fishing in the Shallows."

"I can't wait!" Junius exclaimed. "I can't wait for everything!"

Then he was gone, down the hill and to the dock where his father was already preparing for the trip. His father had his wallet and traveler's checks in a plastic pouch on his shoulder.

"Why you carry that?" Junius asked him.

"You always carry some money, Junius. I use a plastic pouch because on a boat, things can fall overboard," his father said. "This way my wallet or my checks are safely wrapped. Even if they don't go in the water, they won't get wet from spray."

"I see. Do you know how to drive a boat?"

"Well, I'm studying this motor. It's been some time, but I think I know. But that's not the big problem. The big problem is docking this boat at the town dock at the head of the bay."

"That's a problem?" asked Junius.

"It could be, for a man who hasn't done it in some time and if there are a lot of boats tied up. You don't want to hit another boat, Junius. And I'll need your help. So we'll take it slow here and let me think a minute."

Junius waited, watching his father closely. Damius was studying the motor, practicing lowering it from the rest position, which allowed the shaft to remain out of the water, to the running position with the shaft and propeller in the water. Once he had the hang of it, he put the motor in the proper running position. He tested the screws that held the motor to the dory's reinforced transom.

"I've seen a whole thousand-dollar motor topple into the deep," he told Junius, "just because it was not mounted tightly enough. It's amazing Father has done so well. It must take him a long time to get things right before he leaves the dock. Now."

"Now, what?" Junius said.

"Here's what you have to do for me," his father said.

"You climb up on the prow and get back on the dock. Untie the mooring line and hold on to it while I pull up the anchor. We want to keep the dory just where it is for the moment. Whatever you do, don't let go of the line."

"Why?" asked Junius.

"Because if you let go and the anchor is up, the current will push us into shallow water by the shore and the mangroves. We'll be stuck, and a heavy wooden boat is very hard to get unstuck from a mud bottom."

"I see," said Junius. "All right." In a moment, he was on the dock. He had balanced himself pretty well. And he had the line firmly in his hands.

"Okay," said his father. He pulled and pulled, and slowly the anchor came up.

"Never saw an anchor like that," Junius said. Admittedly, he hadn't seen many anchors. Besides being muddy, this one was, well, different from the ships' anchors he'd seen pictures of.

"It's a Danforth," his father said. "You can recognize it by the pointed, V-shaped flukes." He dipped the anchor in the water and shook it to get the mud off. Then he pulled it into the boat and carefully placed it out of the way on the floor.

"Huh," said Junius.

"Now," said his father, "I'm going to start the motor and put it in neutral. You walk with the line to the end of the dock out there."

"Yes," said Junius, watching every move his father made.

His father checked the red gas tank flush up against the stern beneath the transom. He pulled the starter cord and started the motor. The fast putt-putting racket filled the cove with noise. His father shouted, "Now, walk it!"

Junius walked gingerly with the mooring line to the end of the dock, and the dory turned its bow toward him and slowly followed.

"Now push the boat away," his father called. "Keep holding the line but push the bow away from the dock. Get ready to jump aboard."

"What?" But Junius understood, although the idea of jumping aboard a dory that was moving out and away from him was not to his liking. "Where do I jump?" he hollered to his father.

"Onto the prow!" his father hollered back. "I'm kicking it in!" The motor droned and the boat heaved suddenly, reversed, and moved slowly away.

Junius understood very quickly. He jumped onto the moving prow with the line firmly in his hand, as the prow cleared the dock. He sat down hard on his backside. "Ow!"

His father grinned. "You'll get the hang of it," he said. It was necessary for him to yell to make himself heard above the motor. "You'll get the hang of it! You did that pretty well." He put the engine in neutral and then forward, and they headed out, past the dock into the open cove.

"Thanks," Junius muttered. He sat down gingerly on the cross seat in the middle of the boat.

"Too much weight in the back—see how the bow is sticking up?"

"Yes," said Junius.

"Move up another seat toward the front," said his father.

Junius moved up. The boat rode more evenly on the water, and they settled back to begin the journey into town. It was a remarkable ride. The dory went at a good clip. The swells and waves were good-sized, not as small as they looked from the hillside. The dory rode them smoothly. But water still slammed into the boat sometimes. It would spray the whole starboard side. And one side of Junius, too.

"Hey, I'm getting soaked!" he called back over his shoulder. He really didn't mind. The sky was ablaze with blue. White, perfect puffs of clouds climbed behind distant hills. The air was so warm and the sun so hot. And yet, there was a coolness on the water. In a few minutes his wet side began to feel chilly.

His father slowed down. Almost at once, Junius could feel the heat on his back.

"This is fantastic!" he called over his shoulder. The bay was serene. He had never seen such a pure blue sky, nor clouds so white.

"I forgot how nice it could be out here," his father said.

"This is surely the only way to travel!" Junius called.

After that, they simply rode and looked. Junius saw everything he had seen before, and more, only this time from sea level. He looked back toward the land and the dock they'd just left. It was hard to judge distance now. He was not used to thinking in terms of water and then hilly land. The Rawlings hillside seemed a good distance. The manor house at the top looked rather beautiful and not abandoned at all. Nothing moved on the green-brown Rawlings hill.

Will Grandfahtha be all right? Junius thought. Will somebody come, bother him? For a moment Junius felt panic. Supposing someone came, stole Grandfather Jackabo away. And he cried out and Junius or his father weren't there to help him. Junius thought of speaking to his father about it, but then thought better of it.

Pirates or whoever they are won't come in the daylight, I suspect, he thought. They wouldn't dare!

He was certain there was somebody up to something. He hadn't had time to speak to his father about it this morning. But he knew, and it would all come clear, he knew it would, as soon as they had all the facts. How they would separate all the facts from Grandfather's fantasies and dreams, Junius didn't know. But they would, and soon, he was sure of it.

At the point where the cove met the open channels of the deep bay, the sea became rough and choppy with whitecaps showing. What felt like a bucketful of sea hit Junius full in the face and drenched him from his neck to his kness. His father slowed the boat more until they bobbed and rocked through the mixed currents into the deep bay.

The bay was extremely wide. Junius gazed south to his right and out to sea as his father headed the dory toward town. He saw a tree, at the mouth of the bay. It was far off and in light, jade-green water but he recognized its gnarled, weathered shape, and his heart leaped. The Shallows! Oh, I want to go there and go around to Medusa Point. Oh, I understand, I know it, as if I'd been there. Grandfahtha! Thank you for your letters, oh, thank you! Nulio! I will see you, maybe this afternoon.

And now began a fine stretch of water and seaside. In a way it was like traveling from the country into a village. Junius could see everything. On both sides and in front of him at the head of the bay were rolling hills, brown and green. Some of the hills had those pastel houses on them. There were the small brown houses on stilts along some of the waterfront. He saw the rim road, the coast road, where he had traveled yesterday, looking down, all along one side of the bay. The rim road was about halfway up on the hillsides.

"I see," he murmured.

Then, on a very high hill before the town, there

were many modern houses like pieces of cardboard and about the same color. Long, low, slanted roofs, on heavy-beamed stilts dug in the hillside. Suburbs.

"What are they?" he called over his shoulder, pointing.

"New condominiums," his father said, "tourists, windsailers. People are discovering how quiet and peaceful is the Snake. And this bay."

There was a dock on the water below the condominiums. Tied up to the dock was a large sailing vessel and three smaller runabouts. Junius saw windsailers at the dock, their brightly colored sails flopping over the dock above the water. Now he saw two windsailers come out of the groves on the far side of the bay. One had a yellow sail with two blue stripes and the other had a red sail with two black stripes. Very pretty, like butterflies skimming the water. They were making their way across the bay toward the condominiums.

Junius loved the idea of windsailing. "Oh, I have to do that," he told himself. "One day, I must have a sail of my own!"

It took them a good twenty minutes to get to the east town dock. The west dock was where the ferry-boat docked. They passed among a number of anchored vessels, all sailers, sloops and yawls and one beautiful old schooner with a black hull. She was called the *Enchantress II*—Junius read her name—and she was lovely to look at, all trimmed in dark wood. The boats were anchored across half the bay in front of what looked to be a small dockside hotel. It was called Villa Bon Ami. There were palm trees on a sandy beach. And blue loungers on which there were vacationers, lazing in the breeze. Smaller boats were tied up to Villa Bon Ami's dock. And people with scuba equipment, coolers, and towels were getting into the boats, bound for the beach.

Damius Rawlings made a slow right turn toward the town dock. Streets curved up and over the hills down to the dockside. Junius watched the town dock swing into position. Suddenly that was exactly how it looked to him—as if the dock was moving, not he and his father in the boat. He felt dizzy and shook his head rapidly to clear it.

Junius son, don't you get sick and spoil everything! he warned himself.

Before his father said a word, Junius was standing and reaching to climb up on the prow. He had the mooring line in his hand when his father said, "We'll come in slow, but you still are going to have to stop the boat with your hands. You'd best jump onto the dock first and bend down and push or hold the boat away so it won't hit. We don't want to bump the dock. This would be a lot of weight hitting."

But they came in fine. Junius leaped onto the dock. The dory came in lazily behind him. He stopped it by pushing against it with his weight. The bow gently nudged the dock.

"Very good!" said his father. "Hold everything until

I can get out and tie another line to the dock." They tied the boat with two mooring ropes. There were no other boats crowding them.

"What do we do now, Fahtha?" asked Junius, once they were climbing the hill into the town proper.

"The police station, to report a missing person," said his father.

Junius kept silent. But he felt uncertain at what they were doing. After all, he and his father had not seen old Burtie Rawlings. They had only heard about him.

So how do we know he exists? Junius thought. Why must you question every small thing? he thought nervously. Angry at himself, trembling with the excitement of it all, he told his mind to just keep quiet.

# Eighteen

It was nearly eleven o'clock, and the town of Lawrence, Snake Island, had risen with the sun, as it did each day. The pastel houses along the hilly cobblestone streets were swept clean. Their doors stood open to the day, to anyone walking by and to the light breeze off the deep bay. Neat, fenced-in yards were a jumble of a bright-rose hibiscus, flowering cactus, and climbing philodendron. White-painted birdcages hung from glowing flamboyant trees. Junius was stunned by the hues—greens, blues, reds, and yellows—of the macaw parrots that were prisoners among the branches.

If you were mine, I would let you free, he thought to them. He gazed inside the houses as he had before, as he and his father passed them. He turned quickly away, before he met other eyes staring at him from the shadowy interiors.

Stores—the groceries, the hardware store, the furniture store—were open for business. The ferryboat had arrived, and a narrow stream of travelers from the big island was thinning out from the streets. Junius felt very proud that he was now a seasoned ferryboater and islander so like those who traveled everywhere using large and small boats.

At this hour Snake Islanders were going about their daily routines. There were a few four-wheel drives about. A few grandmothers and grandfathers on the steps of front porches, keeping an eye on the toddlers and babies while mothers and fathers did odd jobs or went to work, grocery shopping, etc. The heat beating down, the sky, the scent of flowers, everything made Junius' head spin.

His father led the way at a fast pace along a narrow walk. They passed a small post office and a blue concrete building that was called House of No Worries. It looked to be a family restaurant and bar.

They climbed a fairly steep street, at the top of which was the police station. There were two brown jeeps parked in front. Junius followed his father inside and up to a desk where there sat a man in uniform. He looked at them inquiringly as they came in. There were two other men in the rather large room. Ceiling fans lazily moved the oppressive air about.

One section of the room was separated by a glass enclosure. Inside the enclosure, Junius saw a second uniformed man sitting at a switchboard. He had on earphones and there was a microphone in front of him. He appeared to be reading something.

"Yes? May I help you, Suhs?" asked the desk officer. He spoke in a soft island accent. He was a dark-skinned man just like Junius and his father. All the officers Junius saw were dark-skinned.

"We are here to see someone about a missing person," Junius' father said.

"A relative?" the officer asked.

Damius Rawlings stiffened. He was silent a moment. "I want to talk to someone," he began.

"There are forms you can fill out for missing person," the officer said. "Most the times, people turn up. Getting separated on the ferry is most common, and getting to the wrong island follows second. We have a procedure for persons getting separated." He smiled up at them.

Damius shook his head, and then ran his hand rapidly through his hair. "We are not from the islands. We are visitors—"

"From the States, I can tell," the officer said. "We have lots of visitors from the States now."

"May I speak to the officer in charge?" asked Damius firmly.

"Oh, certainly, Suh. Wait just a moment, please," said the desk officer, getting up. He seemed to Junius to be not particularly interested in confronting tourists from the United States.

Doing his job, Junius thought. Is this all the police there are on Snake Island? he wondered. Just three officers? The third one sat by the door, contemplating the bright sunlight outside. He looked at his watch and got up. Then he went outside, climbed into one of the jeeps, and drove away.

The desk officer walked across the room and opened a door in the far wall, closing it behind him. Junius and his father stood by the desk.

"Not a big police station," Junius murmured softly to his father.

"Not a big town, either," his father answered casually. "And it's the only town on the island."

The desk officer came out and beckoned to them. "You may come this way, Suhs," he said, including Junius. Being called "Sir" was a new experience for Junius.

They followed the officer through the door and down a hall to another door at the far end. They were ushered into a pleasant office where the man who was obviously in charge sat at his desk. His uniform jacket had gold shoulder epaulets and gold braid on his cuffs. Seeing such formal attire made Junius suddenly feel shabby.

The man rose as they entered and looked at them expectantly. He did not smile.

"Good morning, Suhs," he said.

"Good morning, Sir," Damius said. "We're visitors here, staying on the old Rawlings Estate."

"Yes, Suhs," the chief officer said. At the mention of the Rawlings Estate, the man nodded. His eyes became ever so slightly veiled. Junius watched him closely and the man held himself even more erect, if that was possible.

"I am Damius Rawlings. This is my son, Junius. We come from stateside."

"Ah, indeed!" said the chief officer. "From the States!" He pronounced it *Stayets*, as had the desk officer. "Welcome to the islands. Welcome to what all and sundry call the Snake. But obviously, you are connected with this island, and that estate. Your name being Rawlings too." All this said with elaborate formality while he shook their hands. He made it appear as though he were not scrutinizing them. But Junius saw that he was. Junius could watch the man closely while his father talked.

"Yes, I suppose you could say that," Damius said. "My father grew up with Burten Rawlings when the estate was a working plantation."

"You don't say!" said the chief officer. "Many an island mahn of generations ago work on that plantation. It tis said that at one time, almost every family of this Snake Island made what living there was to be made right there. My own father, too."

"Interesting," said Damius. There was a subtle pause.

"Ah, excuse me. Do sit down, Suhs," said the chief officer, indicating two chairs in front of his desk.

Junius and his father sat down, but the officer continued to stand.

"I am the Chief of Police, Downing," the officer

said. He pronounced the word Dow-*ning*, with the emphasis on the last syllable. "The island peoples here does call me just Downing or Chief, and so you may as well." He smiled pleasantly. His eyes didn't smile, Junius thought. His eyes remained carefully observant.

Why does he watch us so, Junius wondered, and then hide that he is?

Damius Rawlings nodded. "Chief Downing," he began, "a while ago, my father decided he wanted to come back here from the States, and he did, living with Burtie Rawlings on the old estate. They were boys together, and they seemed to get along in the present, too, until now. But all I have to go on are letters from my father. My son and I got here yesterday. We came because of some disturbing remarks Father made."

"Yes? And what might those be?" asked Chief Downing.

"Well, the first hint of trouble was when my father wrote that he had run into pirates, out on the inlet on the way to Medusa Beach. He said men who were pirates told him to get out. They shoved him, they knocked him down or he fell down. He was frightened, and afterward he kept Burtie Rawlings' gun in the dory."

"I see," said Chief Downing. He looked away, out a large window, his lips pursed.

"But recently," Damius continued, "my father,

Jackabo Rawlings, wrote that Burtie was taken away—he said by pirates. It happened late at night."

Damius paused, to gather his thoughts, Junius supposed. Chief Downing made no move, nor did he say anything.

"Father does have difficulty remembering things, at times," Damius continued. "He forgets things and remembers some things from the long past as if they just happened. Like pirates. He knows Pirates' Cay and that pirates once used this island as a peaceful headquarters."

The Chief smiled and nodded. "This is true," he said. He glanced at Junius and away again as he spoke. "You will find Pirates' Cay of interest, young Suh. We are building an underwater museum there. Tourists will be able to see the marine life of the islands from glass floors."

Junius smiled and nodded, and Chief Downing turned back to Damius.

"So you see how my father could easily mix up history with present reality," Damius said. "But I've concluded that he saw some persons taking Burtie away. And there may be some connection with the house on the bluff, owned by a man named Kostera, I believe."

Junius sighed inwardly with relief. He hadn't known until this moment just what his father believed.

"My father, Jackabo, never has changed his story about Burtie," Damius said. "And it's a fact that Burtie Rawlings has disappeared. Oh, at least eight, ten days ago. That's why we've come to the police—to report Burtie missing."

The Chief stood with his hands at his sides. To Junius, his expression seemed one of curiosity and sharp, penetrating doubt. Or was it minute inspection? Junius wasn't sure.

He doesn't believe Fahtha. The thought came swiftly to Junius. Does he think Fahtha is— Oh, goodness' sakes, he thinks we're up to something! Perhaps he thinks we shot Burtie . . . Grandfahtha shot Burtie with Burtie's own gun. Oh, no!

"Not only is Burtie gone," Damius said, "but his gun is missing from the dory; his binoculars that Father said he used to watch the Kostera house are gone. His furniture is gone, except his bed," Damius went on. "And it appears that somebody came back for the furniture after the time Burtie was taken away, according to my father. So that's it. We'd like to start whatever procedure you have for a missing person."

"Meaning Burten Rawlings," the Chief said.

"Yes," Damius answered.

Chief Downing came over and sat down. He placed his hands flat on his desk and gazed at a point between Junius and his father.

Then, quite suddenly, he looked straight at Junius. Junius almost jumped, the look was so direct. Chief Downing smiled and spoke softly, rather kindly.

"You like this Snake Island, young Suh?" he said. He pronounced it Snek Eye-*lahnd*, heavy accent on the

[ 227 ]

*lahnd*. "Hmmmm?" the Chief asked. "Is it not a fine place to be!"

Relief swept over Junius. "Oh, yes! It tis certainly a wonderful place," Junius said. "I've never been any-place like it. But I have not been many places, dontcha know." He grinned shyly.

"Now this is strange," said the Chief, looking surprised. He stared first at Damius, then back to Junius. "This young mahn speaks with an island accent but he comes from the United States."

Junius grinned. Damius looked uncomfortable. "It tis because my grandfahtha stay with me when I was most a child," Junius said. "I learn everything from him while my parents work, and my fahtha further his education at night, too." He thought: I learn a way of speakin', I learn about lovin' the islands that my fahtha want to forget about. "And he have such an island accent," Junius went on about his grandfather. "He does still have it, too."

"Oh, indeed! I understand now," Chief Downing said. "How wonderful, the grandfahtha and the young Suh does be from the islands." He laughed at his joke.

Then the Chief turned serious. He shook his head. "We can't keep the young peoples, dontcha know, Suh." He was speaking to Damius now. "There be nothing much for them heah, although the Snake be so nour-ishin' to the souls of them. Most the people own no land anymore. They rent the houses and the fields, too. There is one small industry for making thermostats. But it tis a one-level business, dontcha see. And so the young, they go away."

That's what happen to you, Fahtha, Junius thought. You went away, just like the young of today.

"And white peoples come," the Chief went on, quietly, gazing somewhere between Junius and his father. "Do you know, we have a floating, weekend, holiday boat, and tourist population of nearly five thousand peoples? Can you imagine that, for such a one-electric-light town as this Lawrence?" He chuckled. "With the electricity goin' out at least once every day. And no place to dispose of so much garbage. It pollutin' our beautiful bay. And me with only five policemahns, counting myself? And one doctor—the sailors have taken to calling him Doctor Dead—and one male nurse? Oh yes." He had turned serious again. "And the tourist bring their money and that's good for the Snake."

Junius listened, hypnotized by the rhythmic island voice that was now very soft and steady. Neither he nor his father dared interrupt.

"And their power motors get stolen, too, right off their boats at night," the Chief continued, "and they come to me, hollerin' bloody hell about the thieving populace!

"But they buy up what they can, all the land that was once grazin' land. They sit on their fine vessels and drink and watch tele*vision* and shoot the land price sky high. And it make the black young peoples sad they not got enough money. The black children, they go away. . . ." The Chief's voice trailed off.

Suddenly it was clear to Junius: Fahtha, leavin' and givin' up everything, even the island way of speakin'. Because it hurt him so much to see them that had everything when he have nothin', and no way to get somethin'.

Chief Downing looked momentarily embarrassed at having spoken so freely to them. But that look soon disappeared. After all, he was the Chief, his proud bearing seemed to say. And the Snake was his island.

"I have news for you," he said, rather stiffly. He wrote something on a pad, then pressed a button on an intercom on his desk.

The desk officer came immediately. Without a word, the Chief handed him the note. The officer left.

The Chief was quiet. He set erect, almost at attention, as though waiting. Junius looked up at the Chief; he looked around. The silence grew uncomfortable. He looked questioningly at his father. Damius cleared his throat.

"Chief Downing . . ."

The Chief cleared his own throat and said to Damius, "I have met your fahtha."

"Really?" Damius said. "Well, I didn't realize—"

"Yes, indeed," said the Chief. "And an island mahn he is, too."

Damius waited for him to continue with more details. But Chief Downing remained silent. Again, the quiet grew too long.

Suddenly the Chief leaned toward them and said, "Burten Rawlings is not a missin' person. Burten Rawlings has not disappeared at any time from this island. Burten Rawlings is right here, livin' not five minutes away from this police station."

"Wh—what?" Damius looked stunned. "But . . . I don't understand—"

Chief Downing said, "Burten Rawlings ask me to go check on the old island mahn, your fahtha, Suh. And I did so. I find him sunning himself, one day. He look like most any old island mahn, dontcha know. And Burten told me that the island mahn have relatives who would be comin'. Meantime, Burten would let him stay at the estate. So, you see, I expected some of the old mahn's people. Course, I did not know he was your fahtha, Suh. But he seem all right to me for the time bein'. I leave him there. Yet I make a note to keep a watch on him, in case his people don't come."

"You say Burtie asked you to check on him? But why?" Damius asked.

"Burten Rawlings buy himself a small house here in Lawrence," Chief Downing answered. "He havin' come into an inheritance, dontcha see. Now he has a jeep he buys. He buy furniture, bed, refrigerator, stove. All things he need for town livin'. Burten Rawlings seems well off. He tells all that his wife die and leave him impressive monies."

"But how did Burtie know we were coming?" Junius asked.

"He probably didn't know for certain," his father said. "Burtie figured that if he left Father alone long enough, he would have to write to us to come get him."

The Chief smiled to himself. A grim smile, Junius thought.

They heard hurrying footsteps outside. Junius and his father turned toward the door. The officer who had taken the note earlier from the Chief opened the door and forcibly shoved a man inside.

Chief Downing stood, and his formidable presence seemed to secure the room. From his regal height, he appeared to look down his nose at the man who had entered.

The stranger was a white man, who began hollering from the moment he saw who was there. "I want these blacks *off*!" he yelled. "Do ye hear me, Downing? I want these *American Negroes* off my land!"

Lifting one hand delicately toward Damius and Junius and the other hand toward the stranger, the Chief said, "This is Burten Rawlings, Suhs. The very white mahn who is your lost relative. This is Damius and Junius Rawlings, *Suh*. Do meet your cousins."

# Nineteen

There was a charged stillness as Junius and his father sat there, stunned by the Chief's affront. If calling a scoundrel and a bigot like Burtie their cousin was the Chief's joke, it was a poor one.

Apparently offended also, Burtie yelled, "Bite yer tongue, Downing, bite yer tongue off for that! I'm a white mahn, and proud to be. I tolerate no colored relatives. And I won't have these black devils ruining my land!"

"You watch *your* mouth, Suh," Downing replied. "Lower it down, now."

"Well, I want these . . . these American Negroes off my land. Do ye hear? And they can take Stinking Black Jack with them. I let him stay for old time's sake. He was my servant once."

"That's a lie!" Damius Rawlings said. "My father was never anyone's servant."

Burtie Rawlings went on as if he hadn't heard, as

though no one had spoken. "But Black Jack's worn out ee's welcome. They're all trespassers now and I want them off as soon as can be!"

Burtie Rawlings, Grandfather's old friend, Junius thought, fleetingly. Hard to believe he has the nerve to speak so in front of Chief Downing and us, too. Maybe it's all an act.

Damius Rawlings had similar thoughts. "Some think the surest argument is deception," he said to the Chief, "and the best defense a sudden attack."

He stood up to face Burtie. He leaned very close to him so Burtie could not miss seeing him. He and Burtie were approximately the same height and the same build. A genetic strain of leanness and slow aging was clearly the same in both the black and the white Rawlingses.

Damius' hands were clenched. He was angrier than Junius had ever seen him.

There was a look of fear before Burtie raged again, "Do ye hear me, Downing? I want them off! Off! Off!" He stared wildly, straight through Damius.

"Say one more word," Downing said quietly to Burtie. He took his own chair from behind his desk and rolled it toward Burtie. "Sit down," he told Burtie. "Sit right down and not one word more! No more talk of blacks. No talk of whites. Sit you down, mahn, before I *pin* you down!"

"Yer threatenin' me!" Burtie feigned astonishment. "He's threatenin' a mahn of my kind. The unbe-liev-able gall!"

"Your kind!" Damius said. "I left these islands long ago, and my father too, because of your kind!"

Junius saw his father's look and wished he hadn't seen. That look at Burtie of furious despair. There was in it the old problem of the color line. White opposed to black. And the dread and awful anger of the have-nots.

It hasn't changed, has it? Junius thought.

Burtie was hopping around like a rooster with its head cut off. "I'll tell ye something about all black and dirty—"

He never got to finish because Chief Downing interrupted. He pushed Burtie down in the chair. "I warned you, Suh."

"But ye'll take his side, I know ye will," Burtie whined, suddenly. "Acause he's a black, like you. And what is a white mahn to do these days—"

"You make me sick," said Downing quietly. "I take no mahn's *side*."

He turned to Damius. "And you, sit, Suh. I'll have a word with you in a moment."

Reluctantly, not knowing exactly what else to do, Damius sat.

Chief Downing punched his intercom and turned back to Burtie. "I think you have one government check that does not belong to you, hmmm?" Spoken so suddenly and clearly, out of the blue, that Burtie looked absolutely stunned.

"You don't buy a house and house furnishin's with

no government check belongin' to an old black island mahn, do you?" asked the Chief. "Nor from no wife's inheritance. For the wife, she not die, no, Suh. She still livin' in south Florida, quite alive."

He smiled at Burtie, who was now cringing with terror. "I may be a policemahn in a one-electric-light island town," Downing said, "but I does know how to use the law enforcement system."

Suddenly Burtie was all respect and helpfulness. "Listen, Chief Downing, er, Sir," he said, anxiously. "I cashed Black Jack's money for him and I was on me way to take it out to him. I was! When these . . . these . . ." He gulped and began again. "When his boy, here, and his boy's son come to town."

"He took Father's check?" Damius said. "And don't call me boy! He took my Father's money? Chief Downing, I want this man arrested!"

"I want everybody to be quiet now," said the Chief.

"I was on my way out there," Burtie went on anyway. "I swear to ye, I wasn't going to take one solid penny of Black Jack's—I mean, old Jack's money. I mean, only what he give me for room and board. And he give me that himsel, I swear. I never would take it! We got along. I wasn't no thief!"

The door opened and the desk officer came in.

"Hold Burtie, will you?" Downing told him. "In the holding room with him."

"You arrestin' me? I swear to you, I did not take that check!" Burtie pleaded.

"We'll talk, Mistah Burten Raw-leen," said Chief Downing, as Burtie was taken away. "We'll talk."

When Burtie had gone, yelling and swearing all the way, Damius Rawlings was on his feet again. "That man committed a crime and he must be made to pay!"

"I know exactly what Burten committed," said the Chief. "Please, not to tell me my business."

"Well, I wasn't . . . I didn't mean—" Damius tried to explain.

"Suh," said Downing, "you intend to stay on the estate, for how long?"

"Well, obviously, he wants us off—"

"I mean, how long did you plan to stay?" questioned Downing.

"Through Monday. We'd take the ferry Tuesday morning," Damius said. "Our plane leaves at about one in the afternoon. We'll get home about seven Tuesday night."

The Chief nodded.

"But now . . ." Damius began.

"Don't change any plans," the Chief said. "Mr. Rawlings, stay where you are. Give me . . ." He paused, thought a moment. "I will be out to see you in two days."

"Well. But we are trespassing. I guess we should get off Burtie's land as soon as we can," Damius said. "And then, too, there's my father. I'll have to convince him to leave the island."

"Still, you must wait until I straighten out the government check business," the Chief said. "Incidentally, your fahtha will get his money."

He smiled at Junius and abruptly changed the subject. "The young Suh does go to the beach, yes?"

"Well, not yet," Junius said. "We only just got here. But I can't wait to go!"

"Good," said the Chief. "We are very proud of our beaches.

"I'll be by to see you in two days," he said to Damius. "Don't change your plans, Suh. I am askin' you not to."

Damius Rawlings stared at the Chief a long moment. Something passed between them—some sort of awareness. Junius felt that that's what it was.

Damius was nodding at Chief Downing. He understood only that there was something the Chief was holding back. "Well, it is a lot easier not to change our plans," he said.

"Then it tis settled," the Chief said. "Mr. Rawlings. Young Suh. Wish we could have met under pleasanter circumstance. However, we will do our best to make the rest of your stay on this Snake Island a happy one. Have a good time, Suhs, and not to worry about anything."

Graciously, he ushered them out of his office. The desk officer came to meet them and politely led them to the outer door. There was no trace or sound of Burten Rawlings.

They went outside into the bright sunlight and sudden, stifling heat.

"Whew!" said Junius. "Burtie Rawlings! Goodness' sakes, that was somethin'."

"Huh," grunted his father. "I guess they are keeping him. I just hope he gets what's coming to him."

"You think he will?" Junius asked.

"I don't know. It depends on the Chief, I suppose. We'd better get home," Damius added. "But first let's get some snorkels and masks. I saw them in the grocery."

"Really?" Junius said. "We're going swimming?"

"We have the whole afternoon. And I want to forget all this for a while. Let's get moving!"

They got to the grocery just before it closed for the afternoon. Then they hurried back to the boat.

What a mornin'! Junius told himself. He untied the line from the town dock as he had done from the Rawlings dock. At the proper moment, after pushing the boat out, he leaped onto the prow, and they were off. Weaving among all the sailing vessels docked in the bay across from Villa Bon Ami. The boats stayed there until the last day of the weekend, his father told him, when their skippers came to sail them out.

The dory made its sure way into the open bay, where there was space, no boats to bother them. The air was fresh, and Junius felt cool again. By the time they eased into Pelican Cove and were halfway into it, they could see Grandfather almost at the bottom of the hillside. He had seen them turn out of the big bay toward the Cove from his vantage on the forecourt or down at the kitchen.

Old African mahn! Junius thought. You look just like a mahn from there, a shepard mahn, with that staff and that cloak. Where you going! Goin' fishin'? Comin' to meet us. Oh, Grandfahtha. We are goin' swimming!

And when they were close to shore, coming slowly, carefully in, Junius stood up on the prow. For Grandfather to see him and his fine balance as he helped dock the boat.

"Grandfahtha! Grandfahtha! We are going to go swimming! Hurry, Grandfahtha. Watch me dock. Grandfahtha. See? See!"

Grandfather Jackabo saw. He went as fast as he could down to the dock. And by the time his son and his son's son had the boat in, he was there.

"Hee, hee! Ready! Let's go!"

"What about lunch?" asked Damius.

"And my swimmin' trunks," said Junius. "I forgot about that."

"You get the trunks and towels," Damius said. "I'll get the lunch."

"I'll race you!" Junius told his father. "Grandfahtha, you wait here!"

"I will wait!" cried Grandfather Jackabo. "Hurry, mahns! Hee, hee!"

Junius and his father raced up the hillside. Grandfather could hear them yelling and laughing.

Tis so good! he thought. My son and Junius son with me. Oh, it tis so good. Nulio! We does look for you, soon. Be ready!

Grandfather climbed down into the boat. He left his staff there on the dock. He would wear his hiking shorts in swimming.

By the time Junius and his father came back, Grandfather was sitting comfortably, alert and smiling. He had his cloak off and was sunning himself. He had wetted his bald head with water to keep himself cool. Now water dripped down his face in great tears. He grinned at them. Junius laughed.

In no time, they were off. The food—lemonade in a plastic jug with ice, balogna and cheese sandwiches, apples, cookies—was under the prow. Junius and his father wore their trunks. Now Junius put their new snorkels and masks and their towels into the basket.

"See, Grandfahtha? We got you a snorkel, too," Junius told him, as they headed out of the cove again.

"No! Me?" Grandfather said. "Why you need a mask?" he asked.

"You put it down over your eyes and nose. And you breathe through the snorkel that is in your mouth," Junius explained. "The snorkel hose stays above the water so you can breathe freely."

"Huh," said Grandfather. "You can't dive with Nulio and breathe through that little pipe. It ain't long enough."

"Grandfahtha!" Junius laughed. "It's just for surface snorkeling, and for lyin' by the reefs to see fishes."

"Huh!" said Grandfather. "I watch you do it. Then, maybe."

They went to the Shallows. Damius threw out the anchor. There were clumps of rocks about six feet below them. Junius could dive down to the rocks. There, he found a whole world of life. There were sea urchins with long, black spines, which he was careful not to touch. And bottom feeders. Pretty striped fish and bluish-purple fish, feeding on the plankton on the rocks. He would swim straight away and he could see everything around him. A golden-green world, it was, bright with sunlight and him in the middle of it. There were large stretches of Shallows where the bottom was yellow sand. He was always careful. Most of the time he swam with his old sneakers on. Swam through schools of silver fish—sardines!

They moved the dory closer to the tree in the middle of the deep bay. Junius wanted to see it up close. Grandfather held the motor tiller. Sat right there where Junius' father had sat, for only he knew the very narrow channel between the rocks to the tree. He handled the dory expertly, too.

"It looks so easy," Junius said. "Like we could just go straight to the tree, but we can't. It's treacherous because of the rocks."

The gnarled, twisted tree surrounded by turquoise sea gave the appearance of peace and paradise.

"It's perfect to look at!" Junius said. "And we are all alone. It's all ours!" Then he said no more. Nobody said anything. That was the kind of place the immense middle bay was. The single tree sat atop an enormous, submerged sandbar littered with boulders and rocks. If one knew the channel between the rocks, one could anchor on the bar and look beyond the tree to the dark ocean out there. That was exactly what Grandfather Jackabo did.

There was wind in their ears as Grandfather cut the motor and Damius threw out the anchor again. There was bright, clean sunlight over everything. The hills seemed to sing with the wind. Whitecaps crashed into the reef surrounding the island and broke and came in to the sandbar in gentle swells. Oh, it was glorious.

Junius felt far away. He couldn't tell for sure, but it felt like they were moving, spinning. There was absolutely nobody around, and they were far from town and police stations and the Burtie Rawlingses of life. Too wonderful to say words. Junius closed his eyes a moment and thanked his lucky stars.

There was a tap on his shoulder. It was Grandfather, halfway over the side of the boat, beckoning him. He followed. They swam. Junius taught Grandfather to snorkel, to float below the surface with the snorkel hose sticking up in the air.

They walked up to the tree, with water sometimes at the height of Grandfather's chest. Grandfather leaned his head on Junius, and Junius put his arm around him.

They stood together like that. They each had one hand on the tree and one on the other. Silent, looking out to where the dark waters of the Atlantic thrashed to meet the deep-blue waters of the great Caribbean. The Caribbee!

They could hear Damius swimming and sputtering around. It was nice that he left them alone. Then, back into the boat. Damius called to them. "You, two! Dinnertime!" He meant time for lunch.

"Good!" said Junius. His fingers were wrinkled, he had been in the water so long.

"Very good!" said Grandfather. And they swam the few feet through golden, shallow water to the boat.

They had a fine lunch right there in the dory. Junius never would have guessed he could get so hungry just swimming. They stretched out in the boat and sunned themselves. Dozing. Junius hadn't thought to bring his cassette player, but he would, next time. Or his camera!

The sun was all over him. It was a blanket, warm and yellow. Junius was turning black under the blanket. He got so burning hot, he had to dive into the water again. He lay under the blanket, he dived. In all the heat, he thought of snow and home. The cold north of America. Sarrietta. Always, she was there, around the corner of his awareness. He did not mind her there. She did not bother him there. All was peace and ease inside him.

Nulio did not come to meet Junius. He was not seen this day.

Wonder if I'll ever see him, Junius thought lazily. He and Grandfather were contented lazybones when Damius started up the motor. The sun paused above the west hills.

That late!

Junius felt burnt to a crisp and draped a wet towel over his face and chest.

"We have such a good time in the Caribbee!" he murmured, feeling the dory slide gently along.

# Twenty

Junius didn't know what had awakened him. He had
been dreaming the presence of Sarrietta, but he had
not seen her in the dream. He opened his eyes. He
moved slightly and groaned. Every muscle ached, it
felt like. Missing Sarrietta had taken the place of the
delight in sun and sea; it somehow got inside the aching.

What tis wrong with me, am I gettin' sick? No. Must
be the swimming.

He was sore from all the exercise yesterday. He had
used muscles he hadn't known he had. He moved his
legs and groaned again.

But what had awakened him? Then he heard it. That
special sound. Beating blades, whacking the air in a
muffled attack. He figured out that it was a helicopter
moving off. Junius got up, slipped on his sneakers,
ignoring his aches and pains. He heard Grandfather
Jackabo stir as he went out.

It was morning out, not quite sunup. But it was day and pretty. Junius yawned and left the forecourt for the path.

Might go down to the dock, he was thinking, his brain still fuzzy with sleep. He yawned again. See if there are any fishes that are surface feedin'. Ready to catch with my hook and line. All the fishing lines and bait were in a bucket still in the boat. He paused to gaze out over the bay.

All at once Junius jumped back. He crouched low, unable to fathom what he was seeing. What he saw on the bay was unbelievable.

He heard Grandfather Jackabo coming from somewhere behind him.

"The Lord in heaven!" Grandfather Jackabo whispered, coming up beside Junius and gazing out on the cove.

"I'd better get Fahtha!" Junius whispered back, and hurried to his father's room.

Damius Rawlings was just getting up as Junius called him through the screen door. "What is it?" he asked.

"Hurry!" Junius told him. "You're not goin' to believe this, Fahtha!"

"You're right," Damius said, when Junius and he were back on the path with Grandfather. "I don't believe it."

It wasn't real, it couldn't be.

There before them was the same serene cove, the bay and hills. But now lying to, midway into Pelican

Cove, was the most imposing ship Junius had ever seen up close in his life. There were two other boats, a forty-foot cruiser and a smaller runabout. All had a distinctive red band with an emblem—Junius could read the letters on the emblem, USCG—and blue stripe.

Junius turned to his father. He hadn't formed the question when Grandfather Jackabo exclaimed, "It tis an invasion! We're under attack. Gawd, mahns, this just like Grenada! Call the Coast Guard!"

"That is the Coast Guard," said Junius' father quietly. "That's the Coast Guard ensign, their flag there, and that's the American flag there." He pointed.

"But what's going on?" asked Junius.

The Coast Guard cutter was very still in the morning cove. It seemed to grow bigger as the light came over the east hill, to the right of and somewhat behind the Rawlings hillside. "Dah!" Grandfather Jackabo said, pointing out to the deep bay. Another cutter was slowly, silently gliding into view at the headwaters of the cove. It slowed and stopped right there.

"I wish I had some field glasses," Damius said. "Look up there!"

High on the cliff, above the rim road across from them, the Kostera house was the center of activity. Junius did not see anyone who looked like the men Grandfather had spoken about. He did see uniformed Coast Guard men. They were carrying boxes of things out of the Kostera house to a truck that was there at the side of the house.

"It looks like this has been going on for a while," said Damius. "It looks like they've already taken the men and now they're clearing out the house."

"Goodness' sakes!" Junius said.

The Coast Guard cutter in the cove turned slowly, sliding away. At that point they heard what sounded like mortar firing from far off, beyond the Rawlings hilltop.

"Let's go!" said Junius. Then he remembered that Grandfather couldn't move so quickly. "Grandfahtha, I have to run up there to see!"

"Then run. You too, Damius," Grandfather Jackabo said. "I come right behind you, but taking my time, dontcha see. Go on!"

Junius and his father scrambled to the top of the Rawlings hill. The sun was up now. And it was at once very hot. They were sweating and their faces were burning by the time they made the height.

They didn't see much. Two Coast Guard helicopters came in and out of view from behind the high hill across the horseshoe expanse. The Coast Guard cutter that had been at the mouth of the cove slipped away toward Medusa Point. But it had to cross the deep bay and get into the deep channel, the only deep channel around the sandbar and the Shallows. It headed out into the open sea and turned toward the Point. There it would lie to offshore.

"Something behind that hill over there," Damius said. "I remember, there's a very small island. A couple of them, I think. Very dry and rocky, uninhabited. Do you suppose . . ." His voice trailed off.

"They were doing somethin' over there!" Junius said, finishing for him. "Kostera and his men! Fahtha, that was shootin' we were hearing."

"I think it's stopped now," Damius said. "This is something! Serious enough that the Coast Guard had to come."

"What do you think Kostera was doing?" Junius asked.

"I don't know," his father said.

"Wonder why he didn't get away with it, whatever it was," Junius said.

A slow grin spread across his father's face. "Probably he didn't because of a cool, observant police chief."

"We'll have to wait for the paper to come out and read all about it," Junius said.

"There's still no local newspaper, Junius. I checked in the grocery."

"There's not?"

"No, there never was," said his father. "But I'd guess the whole town is listening in on shortwave and talking on their C.B.'s to boaters who have a better view out in the ocean. There'll surely be news from the big island about this. And the city papers are delivered here every day on the ferry."

"We'll know about it soon," Junius said.

"Soon enough, I suspect," said his father.

Junius laughed. "And we got to see it!"

"We certainly did get to see some of it, Junius. We had front-row seats."

"We missed the capture, though," Junius said.

"You can't have everything!" Damius said. They grinned at each other.

Junius and his father went back down the hill, stopping first in the manor house for supplies from the refrigerator. They found Grandfather Jackabo waiting patiently for them at the long table in the kitchen. Obviously, he'd decided not to make the climb to the top of the Rawlings hill.

"Did you see much?" he asked them.

"We saw helicopters, but that's about all," Junius said.

From the screened-in kitchen, they observed the whole cove and part of the bay. The big cutter was at the mouth of the cove now. The runabout was gone. And the Coast Guard truck that had been up at the Kostera house was on its way along the rim road.

For the first time, Junius noticed a large rubber landing craft by the mangroves across the cove. Men were coming out through the mangroves now. They were probably some of the same Coast Guard men who had been up at the Kostera house. They got into the rubber boat and went over to the forty-footer that was waiting in the mixed waters below the Kostera cliff. All the ships moved off out of the cove and out of sight behind the hill.

Junius helped his father with breakfast—English

muffins and an omelette. He talked to his grandfather about what he thought Kostera might have been up to, but Grandfather Jackabo remained quiet. He seemed troubled. And suddenly Junius realized that they had not mentioned Burtie to him at all, nor talked about what had happened yesterday at the police station. Maybe it was better not to say anything until Grandfather said something.

Damius had been watching Grandfather Jackabo. And, as if reading Junius' mind, he said, "Father, I've something to tell you about Burtie Rawlings. Burtie is all right. We saw him yesterday. He's been living in town."

"That heathen!" Grandfather Jackabo cried. "He left me! But I thought I saw them take him."

"Probably they did take him, just as you said, Father," Damius said. "It had to be Kostera up there, and his men. And I would guess Burtie figured out how to let them know he knew about them and get something from them. Enough money to buy him a cottage. He was lucky they didn't just do away with him."

"Probably he got to talking at them before they had the chance!" Junius said.

"They didn't want trouble," said Damius. "It would seem they had a lot to lose. So it was easy enough to give Burtie what he wanted and keep him quiet."

Seeing Grandfather's sad expression, Junius said, "Let's eat, and can we go to Medusa Beach? Spend the whole day."

"We'll see," said his father.

"My Old Enemy!" Grandfather murmured, softly. But that was all. He ate his breakfast. It was good. And it was a pleasure for Junius to see him eat so well at last.

The rubber Coast Guard boat with the capacity for twenty men was lying in the small-boat channel by Serpent's Point. Damius guessed there would be some sort of Coast Guard boat in tiny Magpie Bay, to guard the inlet over to Medusa Beach. By the time Junius and his father and Grandfather Jackabo had loaded the boat for a day of swimming, the whole town, practically, was out in the bay in fiberglass, metal, and wooden boats, trying to get around to Medusa Point to see what was going on.

"The Coast Guard isn't letting anybody through!" Junius hollered back to his father as they were heading out of Pelican Cove.

Damius turned the boat around.

"No, let's watch awhile!" Junius called to him, but Damius shook his head.

Once they were at the dock, his father explained, "Why get in that crowd out there? There're other beaches, Junius. We'll use the jeep."

"I'll bet not as good as Medusa Beach, Fahtha," Junius said, disappointed.

His father only smiled.

"Hee! Hee!" said Grandfather Jackabo. He liked the idea of riding in the jeep again.

They unloaded the boat and loaded the jeep. Grandfather Jackabo waited in the shade. The work took a while, and Junius and his father were wringing wet by the time they were through. At last, finished, they helped Grandfather get settled in the backseat. And they took the jeep along the rim road all the way into town.

Then they were out of town, climbing a high hill. There was mesquite and heat surrounding them. Longhorn cattle. A few men on horseback among the hills, herding, watching over their widely ranging stock.

Very strange, thought Junius. Cowboys, with not a range to roam.

Damius stopped the jeep at the top of the hill. Junius stared at the view.

"How long has it been since you've seen this?" Damius asked Grandfather Jackabo.

Grandfather thought and said, "Seems like a dream, long ago time it was, too." His voice shook slightly. "It must been most thirty years since I see the Snake Lagoon dah and Flamboyant Beach on dah."

The view was gorgeous. Below the hill was a shallow saltwater lagoon cut off from the sea by sand dunes. They shimmered, draped magically with wild coconut palms and banana trees. There were pink flamingos in the lagoon. Other birds all around. The scene didn't seem quite real. It looked like a movie set to Junius, and not a very good one. Beyond the lagoon with its many birds was a picture-postcard beach. It was a mile-long, half-moon, wide, white-sand beach.

"Hard to believe that!" Junius murmured. There were wild palm trees and flamboyant trees with bright-red flowers, and gentle seas lapping at the shore. "It tis unreal, for true."

They went down. The road was a steep incline that wound around the lagoon, through some very jungle-like lowlands. There were mud furrows where once there had been a road beneath overhanging trees. Junius saw great termite balls in tree forks.

It was good they had four-wheel drive, he thought, or they would have never made it through the mud and standing water. As it was, the jeep felt like a bucking bronco.

They entered an entrance area that was a long sweep of sand behind the beach. There were shelters with open pits in the ground for making fires. There were picnic tables and benches all along low dunes amidst sea grapes and other plantings. And then the beach strip, below the last dune. Junius could no longer see the beach, the dunes were so high.

They pulled up to one of the parking areas behind a beach table. Junius was out of the car and carrying their towels and food and his Sanyo to the table.

"This is all new," Grandfather Jackabo said. "It does not seem like the same place."

"They made it more comfortable for people, families," Damius said. He looked pleased.

Junius left them; he couldn't wait. Scrambling down

the dune, through the sea grapes, he found the amazing half-moon beach. It was long, wide, and handsome, set off by blazing trees, blazing sun, and ocean.

"Oh, goodness' sakes, it tis a dream, dontcha know it!" he whispered. He ran down the beach and waded into the clearest, warmest sea in the world. It was a sweet feeling, that Caribbee. He fell onto his back and floated. He dived, only to find that the tide was out and the water was barely three feet deep for a long way out. But that was all right. He came back in for his snorkel. Out there was a large reef. He could see its dark, purplish shadow spread out under the water.

Junius stayed in the water twenty minutes before Grandfather Jackabo and Damius swam out to keep him company. They had their snorkels on, too. All three of them cuddled up to the reef to watch the bright fishes. Wonderful striped black-and-yellow things. Blue ones and green ones, pretty silver ones. Parrotfish of many colors. Lovely, lovely fishes.

Junius had a kind of sea rapture and could have stayed, hugging the reef forever. Here the water became deeper. There were sea fans all around. Junius pointed at a pretty one. Grandfather touched his arm, shook his head. Not that one. Try the other one, over there. Junius had a hard time getting it loose from the reef. His father helped him. He would take the sea fan home. Beautiful, white coral, shaped like a fan. There was brain coral all around on the bottom.

Grandfather was right with him. He dove for a piece

of the coral that really did look like the human brain. Junius was surprised when Grandfather dived. He hadn't known he could do that with a snorkel. It took some getting used to. Grandfather came up with something else pretty in his hand. He took off the snorkel.

"Junius son," he said, "I give you sea money."

"What is it?" Junius asked. The shape was round, disklike, pale, and very delicate.

"Call it sand dollar. It tis an urchin, shaped like a disk. They are not easy to find here," Grandfather said. "There is a beach on the Atlantic side of the Snake where there used to be plenty. We'll go there sometime."

They left the water to eat lunch. Grandfather spent an hour explaining the dangers of the coral and the sea to Junius. All the while, island music from the Sanyo cooled the atmosphere.

"Watch out for little fish that looking just like the sandy bottom, you can hardly see him. Watch him burrow right under the sand and lay there, and you can't see him then, either. Never try to touch him when you do see him, for he is very poison to you. He can kill you. Just lie still floating, looking at bottom, and you will see him."

"You mean, right there, where we were swimmin'? Where we been walking about? Supposin' I stepped on him?" Junius said, alarmed.

"He won't let you step on him. He too smart, him. He burrow, feel your waves comin'," Grandfather

Jackabo said. "The only time he kill you is when you work at catchin' him and touchin' him. Then he will kill you."

"Your Caribbee is not just pretty, Grandfahtha," Junius said.

"My Caribbee does be dangerous. You learn respect of it, Junius son. And watch out for barracuda." Grandfather continued his sea lessons. "They are there where we were, out there by the reef."

"My goodness' sakes, I didn't see nothing!" Junius said.

"You never quite see him, barracuda," Grandfather said. "He out in the shadows, just beyond where you can see. Where the light fades, he stays. But just know he is there." He grinned lovingly at his grandson. "Listen to me, now."

"I am, Grandfahtha."

"Never go too soon too far out, into the reef, where it seems to fall away from you. It does not exactly fall away. It surrounds you. There lurk the barracuda. Very sharp teeth."

Junius shuddered. Damius watched his father and his son, listening. For the first time, he really listened to the lilting, soft way they spoke to one another. For some reason, hearing them made him feel content. He dozed with the sound of them weaving a fabric of restfulness.

Junius and Grandfather walked down the beach. Grandfather pointed out the machineel. It looked like an old, twisted tree, with little green apples. Junius shook his head at the wonder of such a common-looking but very poisonous tree.

They walked a third of the half-moon beach before Grandfather grew tired and they had to stop. They lay down in the surf and let it wash over them, cooling them.

"Ah, wonder of all wonders, my Caribbee," said Grandfather.

Junius carefully gathered tiny, perfect seashells in his hand.

"See, Grandfahtha? These are the young of the shells you send me. Grandfahtha? The shells you send me were all broken."

"I thought as much," Grandfather said. "You never mentioned them."

"I'll bring a whole duffel full of them back, and the sea fan and anything else, the brain coral, too."

Grandfather smiled and felt Father Sun lie on his bald head.

Thus, Junius spent his third day on Snake Island. It was Sunday. He thought of home and Sarrietta. She, like a soft sea foam in his brain. He lay still on the water snorkling, scrutinizing the bottom until he found an ugly, horned thing that he soon recognized as a fish, the same color as the bottom.

Poison! Junius lay there, watching. There was something wonderful about being so close to danger but out of it, too.

I have not sent one postcard! came to him as he forgot the bottom fish and flipped over on his back. He would do that, he would write cards, first thing tomorrow. Grandfather came to lie on his back beside him. They were two dark floats. They were very still, very amused and happy with themselves.

# Twenty-One

Junius talked his father into staying until Wednesday. Here it was Monday already, and it felt like he had just got to the Snake. "It won't matter," he told his father. "We're on standby, anyway. And we can always get a plane from Atlanta, sometime." So he talked his father into it. He tried for Thursday, but his father wouldn't hear of it.

He was in the kitchen, writing his postcards, listening to Hendrix turned down low and hoping to get the cards in the mail today. "I'll get home before they do," he told Grandfather, beside him. "Listen to this: 'Dear Muhtha. I am way over far now! And you will never guess what happened here in Pelican Cove yesterday. You will never guess! Fahtha is fine, so is Grandfahtha. . . .' "

"Tell Jaylene daughter-in-law I think of her," Grandfather told him. "Send her a card for me. Tell her Merry Christmas."

That made Junius pause. Didn't Grandfather realize he was coming back with them? Uh-oh, he thought.

He heard a jeep. When he looked out, he saw Chief Downing climbing the hill. His father was going down to meet him. Junius went out to meet him also.

The Chief saluted Junius and his father. They all three walked up to stand right on the path by the kitchen. Junius liked the way his father and Chief Downing seemed to fall into a respectful familiarity, like kinsmen.

"Good marnin', Suhs," said the Chief. "I said I would be by to see you." He smiled. "You like the show yesterday marnin', young Suh?" he said to Junius.

Junius laughed. He liked the Chief. "Oh, a very fine show it twas, too!" he said.

"Yah, indeedy!" said the Chief. He had on a khaki short-sleeved uniform with khaki Bermuda shorts. He still had the gold braid on his shoulders.

"Another good day on the Snake," he said to Damius.

"Yes," Damius replied. "May I offer you a cup of coffee?" his father asked the Chief.

"Certainly, Suh," he said.

And they went into the kitchen to sit and drink coffee. Junius turned the radio off.

"Good marnin' to you, Suh," the Chief said to Grandfather Jackabo.

Grandfather stared at him a long minute. "I thought I dream you!"

They laughed. "No, I am quite real," said the Chief. "But you were mostly sleeping when I come to talk to you. Well, it was hot. It tis all right, Suh.

"May I speak plainly?" asked the Chief abruptly.

"Yes, of course," Damius said, handing him a cup of coffee.

"Well then, here it tis. There was trouble here, and we have caught the troublemakers. That tis all I am at liberty to say about that. Burten Rawlings was an insignificant part of the trouble. Foolish mahn, too, to conspire with criminals. After all, no mattah what he is, he is a Snake Islander and we knew his fahtha and his grandfahtha." He cleared his throat and continued, "The perpetrators will have to pay and that tis out of my hands, dontcha know. Burten Rawlings is off island now, in Coast Guard custody, as is Gerard Kostera and his fellows."

They all watched him. The silence was complete.

"Burten Rawlings will lose his house in town, and these lands, more than likely."

Again, a silence as Damius searched the Chief's face.

"Now, all this may not take place for a year, perhaps," Chief Downing said. "This land will lie here, waitin' for who knows who to take it over. I intend to see Burten Rawlings, once he is charged. We will discuss this land. We of the island, the island fahthas, the mayor—I have talked to him—should like to see this land stay in the hands of islanders. It can be rented, all the time Burten must pay the price for his folly. It can be bought, I suspect, once he has paid his price. Burten does care for cash, and I am positive he will be good and sick of island life once he is a free mahn again. At least, he will be sick and tired of *this* island."

"I see," said Damius. "And you want to know . . ."

The Chief did not smile; and yet his expression was quite suitably pleasant, and correct. "We of the island think the black Rawlingses have somethin' due them." He spoke earnestly. "We would like you, Suhs, to hold on to this land here. So. I have said my piece."

Damius remained silent, staring into his cup.

The Chief drank his coffee and got to his feet. "How long will you be staying on here?" he asked Damius.

"In a few days we'll be leaving," Damius said.

"You know, back in the States you are but phone calls away from us here."

"I realize that," Damius said. "And I do intend to keep in touch with you."

"Have you enjoyed it here, Suh?" the Chief asked Damius, kindly, Junius felt.

"It has been . . . almost like old times," Damius said. "I almost felt . . ." He paused.

". . . Like it tis your island, your Snake?" Chief Downing finished for him.

"After all these years," Damius said. He looked around, settled on Junius. "I've been wrong to stay away, I think."

Thank you, Fahtha, Junius thought. I love you.

"The Snake stays with you," the Chief said. "It

twines itself around the heart of you." He smiled. "It tis your island, too, mahn. Take it!"

"Yes," Damius said. "I'll . . . I'll have to think," he finished.

The Chief nodded. "And I'll be right here." Shortly, he left them. They sat quietly, hearing the Chief's jeep start up and go away.

"You leavin' so soon?" Grandfather asked Damius then. "When you leavin' soon?"

"This Wednesday, Father," Damius said. "And you're coming with us."

Grandfather looked surprised. He shook his head. "I'm stayin' right here," he said.

"No, Father."

"Yes, Damius son. I stay put, dontcha see."

"Father, you can't stay here alone! Burtie's in trouble. He's gone for good!"

"The dirty heathen," Grandfather said. "It twas the Planter's Punch, make him think he king of the mountain. I told him not to curse the sun! And he curse the sun! And look what happen to him!"

"Father," Damius said, "supposing you go with us now and we come back in July, all of us, Jaylene, too, and we stay for . . . well, a month or more. What about that?"

"Really, Fahtha?" Junius said. "Oh, Grandfahtha. See? We'll come back."

"But it tis so cold in North America. A mahn like me can't stand the cold!" Grandfather said.

"Well, we'll get you an overcoat. It's because you insist on dressing as if it were still summer back there when it's winter," Damius told his father.

Grandfather laughed and boxed Junius' ears. "You wear my muffla?" he asked.

"I will when we get home," Junius said. "And you will wear the leggings, yes, Grandfahtha?"

"Hee! Hee!" Grandfather said, and then, "Oh, I don't know. I don't know."

"Father, we want you home with us. We all missed you like the dickens while you were gone," Damius said.

"Every day, I would race home to see if there is a letter from you," Junius told him. Shyly, he looked down at his hands on the table. "And Muhtha and I sit and talk about you.

"I turn on the globe each day," Junius went on. "I put it in my room so, 'cause I am missing you so much. Grandfahtha, please say you'll come." Junius gently touched Grandfather's shoulder, and then he scrunched small and put his head on it. He surprised himself; he hugged Grandfather, closing his eyes. He needed Grandfather more than he had ever realized.

Ever so slightly, Grandfather's hands shook as he patted Junius' back. "Big old Junius son!" he said. His chin trembled and he had a hard time keeping the tears from his eyes. He swallowed and the tears went back.

"You miss me, son? I missed you," he said. "I love the sea, but it get so lonely. I forget. I sit on the water, sleep, wake up, and not know where I be!"

Grandfather sighed and seemed to lapse back into his thoughts. Then roused himself. "You want me? You don't want me. I'm old. Too old for anything," he murmured.

"Grandfahtha, where'd you get that?" Junius said, turning to look at him. "I want you! Everybody want you! If you forget things, I'll remind you. If your legs hurt you, we'll put Ben-Gay on them." He buried his face against Grandfather's cheek just as he had as a child. He didn't care if he looked like a baby.

"Big old son!" Grandfather said, holding Junius tight. "Remember, I cradle you when you a very little mahn and have the stomachache."

"Grandfahtha!" Junius whispered.

"Didn't know anybody still care so much, I been gone away so long," Jackabo said.

"You know now, Father," Damius said, smiling. It hurt, though, a little, to see his son closer to his own father than to him. He had a lot of making up to do, Damius thought.

"Let's go swimmin', son," Grandfather said, to change the subject.

Junius raised his head to look at him. "To the Shallows?" he asked.

"Not today," Damius answered for Grandfather. "They're still not letting anybody through. Probably tomorrow will be better. We'll need to pack up tomorrow."

So they spent the day writing cards and fooling around. Grandfather and Junius fished from the dock all afternoon, island music wafting on the air. Damius examined the great house at the hilltop. And he used a machete, cutting through the tall grass down the hillside. He would come back to rest and be with them. Then he would go again. Grandfather and Junius saw him on the road, swinging the machete. Like he somebody knows how, Junius thought.

The next morning Damius was coming home from town in the jeep by the time Junius was up and dressed, and hoping to swing a machete, too.

"Where did you go?" Junius asked him once he was back up on the hill.

"Just into town. I wanted to say good-bye to Chief Downing and make the car reservation on the ferry."

"Oh," said Junius. "I hope you said good-bye for me, too," he said.

"I did," Damius said. "But look here. The paper from the big island. There's a story about us here. We were sitting on a powder keg and didn't know it."

"No kidding?" Junius said.

"Read it."

Junius read. All about Kostera, alias Kotkind, and his men. They were arms and munitions smugglers, they were mercenaries with grand schemes, the article stated. And there were island views of the Snake. And a picture of Chief Downing! Downing had alerted the Coast Guard. And Kostera had been storing huge caches of arms in caves on the small, uninhabited cays near the Snake!

"Goodness' sakes alive," Junius said. "It says they thought about taking over this island—"

"Yes, and supplying arms to anybody they thought could help them," his father said.

"Overthrowin' Snake Island!" Junius exclaimed. "Standin' here, it sounds kind of silly. Who would want the Snake?"

"It would've been a start in this part of the Caribbean, a beachhead. People are poor, I told you that. How could they resist?" his father said.

"But the Coast Guard would never let that happen," Junius said. "Didn't they realize that?"

"The article suggests that they might have been trying to see what they could get away with, and who might be watching a back island," Damius said. "They were confident they wouldn't get caught. Too confident."

"You think they will come back?" Junius asked.

"I think this island and others like it are ripe for trouble, as long as people are wanting and they are surrounded by those who have all the advantages."

"Fahtha! You could come here and run for Mayor or somethin'!"

He expected his father to smile, to tell him he was being foolish. Instead, he looked seriously at Junius. "If I wanted to, I could," his father said. "I come from the islands, too."

Island mahn, Junius thought, he comin' home, I bet you he is!

"The paper doesn't say anything much about Burtie, though, only to state that a Snake Islander had a minor involvement in the whole affair. He's lucky to be alive," his father said.

Grandfather was calling them from the kitchen. When they got there, they saw that he was waiting for his breakfast. Junius and his father went about fixing it. Junius had to run up the hill for provisions from the refrigerator. He could make the run now and not get out of breath.

You should see me now, girl, he thought. Sarrietta, in his head as he ran, and with him constantly now that soon he would be going home. You should know that the Rawlingses are *known* on Snake Island!

Damius showed his father the newspaper article. Grandfather Jackabo glanced at it and shook his head. "What they think, this some banana republic-somethin'?"

"It isn't a whole lot better than that," Damius said.

"Yea, it tis!" Jackabo said. " 'Cause me, you, and Junius son. This is *us*!"

Damius stared at him. "You're right," he said. "It's happening to *us*, this time." And how do we keep it from happening again? he wondered. But it was coming to him. An idea, forming. They would come to the islands often. Maybe it was too late for him to change his life, maybe not. Snake Island! But not too late for Junius. He looked at his son, wondering, and felt good about him. He smiled suddenly, feeling very good indeed about a lot of things.

They ate a too-heavy, but delicious, breakfast of bacon and onion omelette with toast and coffee. The food rested like comfortable weights beneath their belts. It made them long to close their eyes, and it was not yet eleven o'clock.

Grandfather leaned back. He sighed. "And now we go find Nulio in a little while," he said.

"Really?" asked Junius.

"Else we fall asleep," said Grandfather.

"Sounds like a good idea," said Damius. "I mean, going out on the boat—that is what you meant, Father?"

"Oh, sure," Grandfather Jackabo said. "Nulio waitin' to show Junius son how he can swim and sway— hee, hee!"

"But first," Damius said, "what about Wednesday?"

"What? You talking to me?" Grandfather said evasively.

"I'm talking to you, Father," Damius said. "What about Wednesday?"

"What about it?" Grandfather said.

"Wednesday, we must be up very early to catch the ferry out of here."

"Well, I guess I got to go," Grandfather said simply.

"Hurray!" Junius shouted.

"I can't stay here by myself. I can't get around so good no more. I . . . I . . . need help now," Grandfather Jackabo admitted. It wasn't easy for him. He looked down at his empty plate, touched it with his hands.

"We all need help sooner or later, Father," gently, Damius told him.

"I go home with you, my son," he told Damius. "And I go home with you, Junius son, provided . . ." He paused, holding his bald head high. A single tear trembled in his eye. With great effort, Grandfather held it in.

"Provided?" Junius asked.

"Provided what?" Damius asked.

"Provided I, me, drive the boat the rest the time," Grandfather said. He wiped his eyes.

Silence, as they stared at him, and then, "The rest the time?" both Junius and his father said together, island accent and all.

"The rest the time we does be here on the Snake," said Grandfather, stubbornly. "Whether we go in town, in the Shallows, to Medusa Point, *I*, *me*, *I* drive the boat the rest the time."

"*He drive the boat the rest the time!*" chanted Damius. He grinned broadly.

"*He drive the boat the rest the time,*" sang Junius, in his best calypso voice. "*The Snake mahn, the Snake mahn, he drive the boat . . .*"

". . . *the rest the time!*" sang out Damius, in a tinny falsetto.

Junius bounced up and danced around, laughing.

Lo and behold, his father joined him. Damius was a stylish calypso dancer, if somewhat stiff at first. Junius was impressed.

*"He drive the boat the rest the time, any day-o, any day-o,*
*You know him, the Snake mahn. He the Snake mahn,*
*Any day-o, any day-o!*
*He drive the boat the rest the time, mahn . . ."*

They laughed and danced, making up the song as they moved.

"You funny fellows," said Grandfather. "Very funny fellows."

Soon they were seated again. Junius did have writing to do. "Can we go into town on the way back from the beach?" he asked. "I want to mail a postcard to Sarrietta."

"To who?" asked Grandfather Jackabo.

"There've been some changes, Father," Damius told him.

"What?" asked Grandfather.

While his father explained, Junius read over the postcard he had written.

Dear Sarrietta. Hello from Snake Island! I am very over far, as Grandfather says. He is fine now. We are all fine. You will never guess the excitement here. I will tell you all when I return. I get you a fine present on the way. Grandfather coming home with us! Would you like to see Snake Is. when summer come? Say hello to everybody. See you soon! Love, your friend, Junius.

[273]

I hope I'm still your friend, he thought. If not, I will win you back.

"Think of that," Grandfather was saying. "A mahn turn he head one minute and Junius son get a girl-love!"

Junius smiled. "Wait 'til you see her, Grandfahtha!"

"I will certainly wait," Grandfather Jackabo said.

Damius laughed.

Junius found a plastic sandwich bag and put the postcards in it. "Ready," he said. "Let's go find Nulio."

# About the Author

Virginia Hamilton is the youngest child in a large family that has lived in the sweeping landscape of southern Ohio ever since her Grandfather Perry settled there after escaping from slavery in the South. And it was the echoes of her Ohio upbringing—her relatives who became known for telling tall tales, her mother always telling her to "go take a look" at something or someone, her learning to think and to manage childhood feelings in terms of stories—that later jelled into the proper combination of drama and emotional wisdom that makes her one of the finest storytellers of today.

Ever since her first book, *Zeely*, was published in 1967, Virginia Hamilton has gained a devoted following among young readers, and has won every major award or honor accorded to American authors of children's books. Her novel *M.C. Higgins, the Great* won the 1975 Newbery Medal, the National Book Award, the *Boston Globe/Horn Book* Award, and the Lewis Carroll Shelf Award; *Sweet Whispers, Brother Rush* was a 1983 Newbery Honor book; *The Planet of Junior Brown* was a 1972 Newbery Honor book; and nine of her books have appeared on ALA Notable Books lists. As Betsy Hearne writes in *Twentieth-Century Children's Writers*, "Virginia Hamilton has heightened the standards for children's literature as few other authors have."

Ms. Hamilton is married to the distinguished poet and anthologist Arnold Adoff. They live with their two children in Ohio.